Paul McDonald had a corpse . . .

As usual, I parked on Chenery Street across from my house. I admired my paint job, locked the Toyota, and started across the street absently, just performing a familiar act I performed two or three times a day.

I could have admired my own paint all the way across the street, as I sometimes do, but that particular day I decided to compare my house with the Hathwells', two doors down, which hadn't been painted in years. I had to look slightly to my left to do that, and that's how I happened to notice that a car was coming right at me, quite a bit faster than a speeding bullet.

TRUE-LIFE ADVENTURE

Also by Julie Smith

HUCKLEBERRY FIEND

Published by
THE MYSTERIOUS PRESS

TRUE-LIFE ADVENTURE

A Novel by
JULIE SMITH

THE MYSTERIOUS PRESS

New York • Tokyo • Sweden

Published by Warner Books

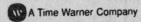

A Time Warner Company

The characters in these stories are fictitious, and any resemblance between them and any living person is entirely coincidental.

MYSTERIOUS PRESS EDITION

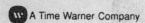 Mysterious Press books are published by
Warner Books, Inc.
1271 Avenue of the Americas
New York, N.Y. 10020

W A Time Warner Company

Printed in the United States of America

Originally published in hardcover by The Mysterious Press.

First Mysterious Press Paperback Printing: November, 1986

Reissued: January, 1993

10 9 8 7 6 5 4 3 2

For Titter

Acknowledgments

The author thanks Dr. Boyd Stephens, John Reid, Susan Price, and Veronica Napoles for help in their various fields of expertise. Paul McDonald extends special thanks of his own to Jon Carroll, without whom he would have been less of a man.

CHAPTER 1 "That stuff'll kill you."

"What? Your coffee?" Jack was just doctoring his second cup.

"No. All that saccharine. You're poisoning yourself."

"We've all gotta go sometime."

Jack went right about then. His eyes rolled back and he let go of the cup. Coffee sloshed all over my rug. His big body fell forward in the chair.

I tried to lift him by the shoulders to get him upright again. I wasn't sure why—I thought I wanted to look at his face or loosen his tie or something. But really I just wanted to undo what had happened, to see him sitting in the chair the way he'd been a moment before.

But I saw how dumb that was and I called 911.

I tried feeling for a pulse; I couldn't find one. So I tried to think of something else I could do, anything. Mouth-to-mouth resuscitation maybe. But I couldn't get him in position. He was built like a bear and I wasn't sure I should move him, anyway. I wound up just standing there by his chair with my hand on his back. My cat Spot rubbed against my legs, sensing I needed comfort, trying to do the same thing for me I was trying to do for Jack. I was grateful.

We were there a long time, Jack and I, like some tableau in a wax museum. I heard a siren and I went to let the paramedics in. They laid him out and attached something to his chest. I went into the kitchen, telling myself I needed to get out of their way. But the truth was, I didn't want to watch. Jack wasn't a friend or even someone I especially liked, but I was afraid he was dead and death makes me squeamish. Or dying does, anyway.

So I stood in the kitchen, patting Spot and staring out the window.

After about a month and a half one of the paramedics came in. He was twenty-fiveish and blond, very innocent-looking. "I'm sorry," he said. "We couldn't do anything."

"I—uh—thanks for trying."

"My partner's calling the coroner's office. We'll wait till they get here."

I said I needed some fresh air and they let me go out into my postage stamp of a garden and sit there until the coroner's wagon came. Then they said good-bye and a deputy coroner came out to talk to me. He said his name was Stanley Smith.

"Paul McDonald," I said.

"And your friend's name?"

"My friend?" I realized he meant Jack. "Oh. Jack Birnbaum. He wasn't a friend, exactly. I was doing some work for him."

"What kind of work?"

"Client reports. Jack was a private detective."

"I don't understand."

"I'm—uh—a ghostwriter."

2

It sounded dumb and I was embarrassed. Sometimes I said I was an editorial consultant. Really I was an ex-reporter trying to make a living free-lancing. I did brochures for banks and how-to books for publishers and autobiographies for rich people who didn't know how to write—anything, so long as you could do it on a typewriter and it wasn't journalism.

I started doing Jack's reports when some client or other dumped him because he couldn't make sense out of them. Jack called the *Chronicle* and tried to hire Debbie Hofer, who referred him to me.

I thought the gravy train had just pulled into the station. Jack would detect all day and phone me at six for what he called "debriefing." Since his verbal skills were pretty wanting, that usually took at least an hour, and I charged him thirty dollars a phone call. Then, at the end of the week, I'd whip him up a client report and he'd work me into his expense account somehow, and everybody'd be happy.

The gig bought Spot a lot of Kitty Queen liver and chicken, but what I liked best was that it was so cute. I could go to a party and say I was a ghostwriter for a private detective and I'd have a crowd around me in about three seconds.

But somehow, telling it to a coroner's deputy in my backyard on a Monday morning, it didn't sound so cute. It didn't matter, though. Jack was the one he was interested in. I told him all about how he was drinking coffee one minute and lying there dead the next.

"Did he complain of feeling sick at all?"

"Yes. Come to think of it, he did. He said he thought he was getting the flu."

"Did he mention any symptoms?"

Something Jack had said came back to me with a nasty clarity. "He said his heart felt funny—like it kept skipping a beat. And he said he was seeing spots."

3

Stanley Smith looked at me like I was a moron. I tried to explain why I hadn't diagnosed heart trouble and bundled Jack off to Mission Emergency: "I didn't think about it much because mostly he complained about his stomach. He said he had the stomach flu."

"Did he eat anything while he was here?"

"Just drank some coffee. I didn't think it was the best thing for the flu, but he wanted it."

"Did he ever talk to you about any heart trouble—any medication he took for any chronic illnesses?"

"No. He seemed fine until today."

"How long have you two been working together?"

"About three or four months." I shrugged, feeling helpless. "I'm afraid I really didn't know him very well."

Stanley Smith left, taking his colleagues and Jack with him. I felt not just depressed, but panicky, as if I didn't dare look back because something might be gaining on me. Jack was fifty-five, which is too young to die, and I was thirty-eight, which is too old, like the man said, to be a young talent.

When I was in my early twenties, I took off to see the world, so that was out of the way. When I was a reporter, I covered the war in Vietnam; the entire Patty Hearst case, including the trial; the holocaust at Jonestown; and approximately fifty-nine thousand soporific meetings of various city councils and county commissions. Nobody could say I hadn't been around. I'd also known lots of women and maybe loved one of them, I think.

But the things I hadn't done were the ones I didn't want to think about, and Jack's death was kind of stirring things up. I was afraid they might start crossing my mind and that's what was making me panicky. If I'd known a woman who was fond of me, maybe I could have called her and she would have made me feel better. But there was no such woman in the world, probably including my mother, and that was one of the things I didn't want to think about.

So I did what I always do when too much reality starts intruding on me—I sat down at my typewriter and made up things. I write detective novels when I'm not ghostwriting. I'd never gotten any of them published, and that, of course, was the main thing I didn't want to think about.

But writing them is what keeps me going. It's a way of making things make sense. My characters do what I want them to and I know right from page 1 that everything's going to come out okay. And nowhere along the way, no matter how many unfortunate incidents occur, am I going to have to smell nine hundred bodies rotting in Guyana and wonder what could have been done to prevent the thing and whether anyone will be punished for it and how much, if anything, can be learned from it.

You've heard about journalists burning themselves out? Too much true-life adventure is what does it. Making things up saves a lot of wear and tear.

That's what I decided when I quit the San Francisco *Chronicle* and became an unsuccessful detective novelist masquerading as a ghostwriter. And now here I was: sitting in my dining room/office, trying to think up trouble for a made-up detective to get into when a real-life detective had just walked into my house and died drinking a cup of coffee. I'm not normally given to writer's block, but this was ridiculous.

I gave up and went to the movies.

When I got back, I was feeling a little better, but my house, which I loved and which was the only thing besides Spot I could call my own, wasn't where I wanted to be. It felt oppressive, as if death had left behind a murky residue. The murk was in my head and I knew it, but I opened all the windows just in case.

Then I put Dolly Parton on the stereo, poured myself a glass of Mondavi Barberone, and got my mind on Dolly's

5

troubles. For such a smart, successful, good-looking woman, she has lots of them, and I can sometimes take comfort in the knowledge. Not that I want Dolly to be unhappy—it just kind of puts things in perspective to know that no one's exempt.

I was on my second glass of the Barberone and feeling its purple glow in my cells and synapses when Debbie Hofer of the *Chronicle* rang up. There *was* a woman who was fond of me. Maybe two, even—I'd probably been wrong about my mother.

"I'm calling about your dick."

Debbie was sixty-three and getting younger every day, apparently. "Sweetbuns!" I said. "I knew you'd come around."

"Jack Birnbaum, you idiot. Wasn't he your dick?"

"Oh. Yeah. I forgot for a minute." What I'd forgotten was that I used to call Jack Birnbaum my dick to amuse my friends. As in: "Gotta go now; my dick's going to call in at six"; or, "Yeah, I'm making it okay; I've still got my dick." What a card.

"The cops say he died at your house."

"You doing his obit?"

"Yeah. What was it, stroke or something?"

"Heart attack, I think. 'Died suddenly' ought to do it."

"What was he doing there, anyway?"

"Picking up one of my handcrafted client reports."

"Oh, God. Don't tell me he didn't pay you before he conked out. Look, if you need any money—"

"Thanks, Deb. I'm okay."

"You want a mench?" A mench is a mention in Debbie-speak. It was sweet of her, but I didn't want to steal any of Jack's glory.

"No, thanks. How about 'died suddenly at the home of a friend'?"

"Okay. Let me know if you need a loan."

When I hung up, the purple glow was fast disappearing.

Though with the best of intentions, Debbie had brought up yet another subject I didn't want to think about. Jack hadn't paid me before he conked out. He owed me $250, which would have doubled my fortune.

Somehow, in the previous month or so, no banks had needed brochures and no egotistical rich people had needed autobiographies. Jack was my last and only client. I literally didn't know where my next dime was coming from.

I drank a lot more wine before I went to bed that night and still didn't sleep very well.

I got up early. I was sitting on my sofa, reading Jack's obit, when the doorbell rang. I threw the *Chronicle* down on the coffee table and opened my door to Howard Blick, a guy I knew from my days on the police beat.

He might possibly have achieved some measure of success as a hod-carrier, say, or a tube-winder. Unfortunately, some bozo with even fewer brains than he had had made him a homicide inspector for the San Francisco Police Department.

I didn't like him and he didn't like me, but he was on my doorstep and my mother brought me up right. I asked him in and offered coffee.

"No, thanks," he said. "That's what Birnbaum was drinking, right?"

"For Christ's sake, I didn't poison him, Howard."

"Somebody did."

It took me a second to catch on; I'm a little slow in the morning. "They did the autopsy already?"

"Yeah. Digitalis poisoning."

"Digitalis? The heart stuff?"

"Yeah, but he didn't have heart trouble. He had no reason in hell to take it and no prescription for it. Somebody croaked him."

"And you think it was me." This might seem like

7

jumping to conclusions, but you have no idea how dumb Blick can be.

"Well, now, there's a little mystery about it, McDonald. And mystery's what you specialize in, right? You still writing that trash?"

"What are you getting at, Howard?"

"There's a couple of little tricks to killing somebody with digitalis. Not everybody would know how to do it. Maybe a mystery writer would."

"Not this one. But if I wanted to know, I'd call up the coroner, say I was writing a book, and ask him."

"Somebody did."

"Huh?"

"Somebody did, exactly like that, about a week ago. Dr. Blankenship thought it was kind of a coincidence. Seems when you do an autopsy, you've got a choice of certain tests you could do or not do, depending what the first tests show. You follow?"

"Barely."

"Well, early on, this one started looking like a toxicity, so Blankenship did the test for digitalis. When it turned out positive, he remembered the phone call."

"Was the caller a man or a woman?"

Blick looked confused. He'd probably forgotten to ask. "The point is, it's the sort of thing you'd do. And you know what else? Digitalis has an alkaloid taste."

"So?"

"So you couldn't taste it in coffee. That's one of the little tricks to pulling it off. Also, it's not very soluble in water. But the heat of the coffee would increase the solubility."

That was supposed to tighten the noose and scare the hell out of me. What it did was shift my famous quicksilver brain into gear—I remembered why Jack and I had been having that little talk about saccharine being poison.

"Don't tell me what the other trick is. Let me guess.

8

One tablet wouldn't kill you, right? You'd have to get somebody to take them for several days."

"Bingo, McDonald. Now how'd you know that?"

"Like I said, Howard. I guessed." I swept the *Chronicle* off the coffee table. Underneath was Jack's little bottle of saccharine, right where he'd left it. "See that? It was Birnbaum's. Ready for my second guess? Have it analyzed and you'll find some of the pills are saccharine and some are digitalis."

Blick's face was as flat as his feet, and right now his eyes were practically hidden under great hooded lids. He looked more like a potato than a man. I had a chance to observe all that while he was gathering his meager wits. The potato spoke, or rather blurted: "How do you know that?"

"Little gray cells, Howard. Simplicity itself. Birnbaum kept saying my coffee was lousy. Then he said everybody's coffee'd been tasting lousy lately and he guessed it was the flu he had. He was using a lot more saccharine than usual. From that I deduce that everybody's coffee tasted bitter when he put digitalis in it and that made him keep putting pills in till he hit enough of the saccharine to sweeten it."

"Deduce, shit! Maybe you know because you put the pills in the bottle."

"Howard, come off it. If I'd done that, I would have poured the contents of that bottle down the toilet the minute my victim was dead, then thrown the bottle out." He looked doubtful. "Look. Jack always carried that saccharine bottle with him. He always used it to sweeten his coffee and he always drank two cups—in fact, that probably explains how he happened to die when he did. He'd just finished one cup and was starting on his second—that means he'd probably just gotten a blast of digitalis.

"The point is, he always put his saccharine bottle on the

9

table and left it there to sweeten his second cup. And he always picked it up just before he left and put it in his pocket again. At least that's what he always did here, and you can ask his wife if he did it everywhere. I'm betting he did, and that means anybody he'd seen in the last week could have substituted a doctored bottle."

"They'd have had to know his habits."

"I expect the murderer was someone he knew, Howard. A perfect stranger would hardly have a motive, would he?" I was just about out of patience and I guess my tone of voice was a little on the sarcastic side. Even Mr. Sensitive couldn't help noticing.

He said: "Don't get smart with me, asshole."

And I said: "Don't accuse me of murder, douchebag."

"Maybe you've got a motive."

"Come on, Howard. He was keeping me in typewriter ribbons. The minute he stopped breathing I stopped having an income."

"Yeah. Stan Smith told me about that. What case were you and him working on?"

"That's confidential."

His gray-green complexion got suddenly rosy. "Confidential, hell! This is a murder investigation. He was here to pick up a report, right?"

"If you say so."

"I want it."

"So get a search warrant."

He picked up the saccharine bottle and stood up. "You better watch your step, asshole."

I hate being called an asshole in my own house, and that was twice, but I let it go. I'd baited him and I shouldn't have.

All the same, I didn't think I was impeding a murder investigation. The case Jack and I were working on was pretty routine. It was a custody case, the sort that keeps private investigators in business now that California has no-fault divorce. The way it works is, one parent gets custody after the divorce, then the other parent gets mad and snatches the kid, and the one with custody hires a P.I. to find his little darling.

The only thing that made this one any different from a million others was that the *Chronicle* would have put it on page 1 if they'd known about it.

CHAPTER 2 Jack's client was Jacob Koehler, the Nobel prize-winner, the guy who put genetic engineering on the map. The snatcher was Lindsay Hearne, local television's hottest property and Koehler's ex-wife. The kid was seven-year-old Terry Koehler, who'd been living with her daddy and his nice new wife for the last couple of years.

One Saturday about three weeks before Jack died, Lindsay picked up her daughter Terry for a weekend visit and didn't return her on Sunday night.

That was the whole megillah. Great name recognition, but no obvious murder motive.

I was pondering the thing when the phone rang. It was Ben McGonagil of the brand-x paper, the one that comes out in the afternoon. He wanted to confirm that Jack had indeed died at my house and also he wanted to shoot the bull and pump me about Jack. I thought if he gave me a

13

mench, the remaining P.I.'s in town might beat a path to my door and I could go on feeding Spot.

So I told him all about being Jack's ghostwriter and nothing about the Koehler case. Then, since I didn't have any clients to work for, I went back to Chapter 10 of my latest unpublished masterwork.

However, the muse did not sit on my shoulder. I sat there for two hours trying to get my hero out of a jam. It wouldn't have been so bad except that I couldn't think of a jam to get him into.

Normally I don't smoke, but I went out for cigarettes. While I was at it, I decided to grab a bite, and while I was at that, I read the *Examiner*, which was hot off the presses.

McGonagil's story was on page 1, and I was in the fifth paragraph, describing how poor Jack had rolled back his eyes and fallen over. My mench wasn't exactly what I'd hoped for, though. McGonagil said I was Birnbaum's "assistant."

No doubt he thought I'd get a kick out of it, but it wasn't going to sell any client reports.

I was still brooding about it when I got home. I parked on Chenery Street across from my house, admired its terra-cotta paint job, and wondered how I was going to make the next mortgage payment.

Spot met me at the door and I turned my mind to his future health and welfare; I even bent down to pet him, I felt so guilty about being a lousy provider.

But I told myself at least he had a comfortable place to live, with a blue-green sofa to curl up on and lots of sunny places to take naps in. The living room opened right onto the dining-room/office, which had French doors opening onto the garden, so it was always bright inside unless it was foggy outside. My combination dining table and desk stood in the center of the second room and it was the only piece of furniture in there. Otherwise, the room was a greenhouse—a perfect little jungle for a medium-sized black cat.

I surveyed it smugly. And that's how I happened to notice that a pane in one of the French doors was broken.

I made a rapid-fire assessment of the living room. The blue-green sofa was there, and the rocking chair and the bookshelf. The Maynard Dixon painting still hung over the fireplace. The stereo was still on the little low table I'd made for it. The old wooden trunk that I'd refinished was in its accustomed corner, but there was a nice clean square on top with lots of dust around it.

My TV had been in that square an hour ago.

Quickly I went upstairs to check my camera. I was betting it would be there—if the burglar hadn't bothered with the stereo, he probably wasn't going to go look through a bunch of drawers. I was right.

It was a hit-and-run burglary, and it was yet another example of the way my life was going. I couldn't help thinking that, even though I ought to have been grateful about the stereo and the camera.

I called the cops and waited. And waited some more. After about half an hour I grew restive. But I waited another twenty minutes.

Then I couldn't stand it anymore. I didn't know anyone in burglary, so I called Blick.

"Howard? McDonald here. I've been burglarized."

"So call burglary."

"I did, dammit. About an hour ago. Nobody's turned up."

"And you want me to goose them."

"I'm not asking for any special privileges. I just thought you'd want to know."

"Maybe if you'd cooperated a little better this morning, you wouldn't be having this problem."

"Are you saying this is deliberate?"

"I'm just saying people get what they deserve. Probably

someone else in Glen Park has an emergency, but maybe the other emergency wouldn't have happened if you'd been a better sport, you know? It's like karma."

I hung up and waited another half hour. And then Officers De Silva and Partridge turned up. They looked at the undusty square and the broken French door.

De Silva spoke: "Kids. They'll probably sell the TV to some relative for about ten bucks. Zero chance of recovery."

"Well, how about prints?"

"Prints?"

"After they broke the glass, they had to reach through the door and turn the knob. There might be prints on it."

Partridge walked over to the door, grabbed the knob, and opened and closed it a few times, obscuring any possible prints. "Yeah," he said, "I see what you mean."

"You guys must be pretty good friends with Inspector Blick."

"He said you were a real true-blue friend to the department," said Partridge, "and we should do anything we could to help you."

"Thank him for me, will you? For taking such an interest in my karma."

So that's how Blick got revenge. Probably I'd tipped him to a great opportunity when I called him. So it was partly my own fault, but that only made me madder. I vowed to break his jaw if I ever saw him again.

I got my chance at eight A.M. the next day, Wednesday, when once again I opened my door to his ring. But, hell, my mother brought me up right. I asked him in and offered coffee. Some people never learn.

"Jeez, McDonald," he said. "You got a hell of a gut. You ought to take up racquetball or something."

What a prince. I thought I cut quite a figure in my blue jockey shorts, which I had pulled on upon rolling out of the rack. I also thought any jerk who got me out of said rack at that hour had a nerve running down my conformation.

"Blow it out your ass," I said.

He didn't miss a beat. "You have the right to remain silent. You are not required to say anything to the police at any time or to answer any questions. Anything you say can be . . ."

"What the hell do you think you're doing?"

"I'm arresting you, asshole. Insulting an officer, using obscene language, and indecent exposure."

"Indecent exposure! This is my house, douchebag."

"Anything you say can be used against you in court. You have the right to talk to a lawyer . . ."

"Okay, Howard, I'm sorry. I apologize, okay?"

"That's better."

"You want coffee or not?"

"I want the file on Birnbaum's case." He shoved a search warrant in my face.

"Why didn't you say so, Inspector? Glad to help out. Dee-lighted. Any time I can be of service don't hesitate to call on me."

I was delighted. The file wasn't going to help him one whit, and I'd made him go to the trouble of getting a search warrant and making an extra trip and that was payment for calling me an asshole the first time. Now all I owed him for was the remark about my torso, two more "assholes", and the sympathetic assistance of Partridge and De Silva.

I went to my file cabinet and started rooting around. I looked between Bank Statements and Brochures. No joy. So I looked in front of Bank Statements and behind Brochures.

No Birnbaum.

"Just a second, Howard. I guess I've misplaced it."

I went through the whole goddam drawer, but I knew I

17

wasn't going to find it. I could remember putting the file back, just so, after Stanley Smith left with Jack's body.

"Howard, we've got a problem."

"You got a problem, McDonald. I got a search warrant."

He started pulling pillows off the sofa, books out of the bookcase.

"Howard, wait a second . . ."

He opened the trunk where the TV used to be. He started throwing papers on the floor—pages of novels that hadn't been published. The editors of the world didn't like them, but they were all I had to show for my life.

He was making me mad. And when I get mad, I get stubborn and childish. I know because sixty or eighty women friends have mentioned it in passing.

So I let him rip.

I could have stopped him, reasoned with him, told him about the Koehlers, let him go look up Jack's copy of the file, parted friends. But I didn't. I let him tear my house apart because I knew he wouldn't find the file and it would frustrate the hell out of him.

One day maybe I'd grow up. If I did, that would entitle me to call all the women in my past who'd said they might consent to, say, have lunch or something when it occurred. It could have been a real boon to my social life. But it didn't happen that day.

Blick wasn't the soul of emotional maturity himself. There was simply no need to empty Spot's litter box on the kitchen floor.

Naturally, he didn't find the file because it wasn't there to find. If I'd gotten a little more cooperation on my burglary, I might have pointed out the obvious—that whoever had taken my TV had done it only to make the thing look routine.

The point was to steal the file.

CHAPTER 3
Whoever had stolen it apparently hadn't known about me until McGonagil's story came out in the *Examiner*, identifying me as Jack's assistant. And then he hadn't wasted any time. So it looked a lot like Blick was right, after all—the murder had something to do with the Koehler case.

But maybe not. There were about eight other cases in the file. How could I be sure the Koehler reports were the ones the murderer wanted?

And why should I care, anyway? I was thinking like a journalist, a habit I thought I'd kicked.

But the murder had been committed in my house, and my house had later been burglarized. That meant someone had committed two outrages against me, Paul McDonald. That was why I should care.

I knew an easy way to find out the answer, but I needed professional help. I phoned Booker Kessler.

Booker was a little squirt about twenty-six years old,

19

five feet six inches tall, and 135 pounds heavy. He had curly red hair, freckles, and usually a gorgeous woman on each arm. I never saw a guy that did so well with the ladies—he must have been nonthreatening or something. Either that or he was hung like a Clydesdale.

He wasn't home. He kept extremely irregular hours, so he could have been anyplace in San Francisco, but I was betting he was having a long lunch with a lovely. I called Perry's, the Washington Square Bar and Grill, and McArthur Park, which was where I found him. I told him to wait for me.

When I got there, he was lounging amid the wicker and ferns in jeans and a T-shirt, looking about twelve. His companion was Asian, permed, silk-jumpsuited, and red-lipsticked. She looked like she was babysitting.

Booker jumped up. "Paul! It's great you could join us."

"Booker, I need a favor."

"Sure. Absolutely. Meet Denise. Denise, this is Paul McDonald, the writer I was telling you about."

Denise smiled and gave me a look that said she'd be just thrilled to spend the afternoon committing unnatural acts; I didn't think it meant anything, it was just a way she had when she wanted something.

"Denise wants to be a writer," said Booker happily. "Paul, what are you drinking?"

"Gin and tonic," I said, and tried to look pleased. I wasn't. I wanted to get on with business. Booker owed me, but all the same, he was apparently planning to extract a favor for my favor—I was going to have to sit there for an hour or two and give Denise job-hunting ideas.

Now you might not think an hour would be that important, considering I wasn't on too tight a schedule, and maybe it wasn't. But I was impatient and I hated doing dirty work. This was going to be dirty work: I couldn't tell Denise the truth because Booker wanted me to make her happy and the truth about journalism wouldn't do that. On the other hand, if I were somehow responsible for her getting a job on the *Chronicle*, that would make her miserable and I would have it on my conscience.

I plunged in, hoping she wasn't talented enough to get a writing job and ruin her life. "What are you doing now, Denise?"

"Working at I. Magnin. In the cosmetics department. And I'm registered at a couple of modeling agencies, but you can't support yourself modeling in this town."

That boded well. She'd probably never touched a typewriter and never would. I'd met plenty of people like her, people who were unhappy with whatever they were doing—driving a cab or tending bar or being mayor—and thought they'd go into writing one day. They never did and lucky for them—I was willing to bet Denise had made more from part-time modeling in the last month than I had from writing in the last year.

So I gave her a couple of names of editors to look up, told some hilarious newspaper anecdotes, and didn't tell her I'd happened to meet Booker on a story. I didn't think he'd want her to know about that because the story was all about how a kid from the right side of the tracks got into burglary. Booker thought that, in his case, it had something to do with the fact that his mother left his father for another woman about the time he was starting to shave. He was in analysis.

Anyway, I must have been suitably amusing because pretty soon it was almost the cocktail hour and Denise had another date. Booker did too, but he agreed to put it off for a couple of hours.

We went to the men's room while I told him what I wanted.

"Easiest thing in the world," he said. "You can do it yourself. See, you just take your Visa card and . . ."

"I need moral support." Also, I didn't have a Visa card.

21

When the Visa people closed my account for nonpayment, I cut my card in a zillion little pieces, smeared them with cat food, and sent them to Visa central. So I was a little short on burglary tools.

But I wasn't going to have to tell Booker all that and I knew it. In the first place, he owed me—not only had I set Denise on a new career path, but I'd also posted bond for him once. In the second place, he loved his work.

Jack's office was on Kearny Street, in one of those two-elevator buildings you can miss if you don't pay strict attention to the street numbers. I can say this with perfect confidence because Booker and I were gassing a bit and in fact we did miss it. That's how relaxed Booker is about his job.

There was nobody waiting for the elevator, so we took it to the fifth floor. Jack's office was on the fourth floor, but Booker said you always had to walk down one in case somebody was waiting for the elevator on the floor you wanted. If you got out and walked past them, they might remember you.

So we walked down and nobody was on the fourth floor, at least in Jack's corridor. It was an empty white tunnel with a wine-red carpet. Jack's office was number 443. The lettering on the door was very discreet—"Jack Birnbaum," period. Not "Jack Birnbaum, Ace Private Dick" or even "Birnbaum Investigations." Just "Jack Birnbaum." Maybe he'd had more class than I gave him credit for.

Booker tried the door, found it locked, and shrugged. "Half the time they're open," he explained, not even whispering. This job was a piece of cake for him, but parts of my Xtra-large front-pocketed Western-style shirt were getting a little clammy. I wished he'd shut up and get on with it.

My wish was granted instantly. Booker simply reached

in his pocket, pulled out a key, and opened the door. I was impressed. "How'd you do that?"

"Luck," he said, stepping into the office. I stepped in too and we closed the door behind us. Booker turned on a light and held up a key ring with about fifty keys on it. He turned three of them up. "I knew it had to be one of these, and I happened to guess right on which one."

"Do you always carry all those keys?"

He thought a minute. "Not if I'm going to the beach, or playing tennis. Never jogging or sailing, and rarely cruising bars. Other than that, yes. You never know when you might pass a tempting little setup."

"Glad I could oblige you."

"Next time make it a little tougher, okay? These easy ones are bad for morale—I mean, you might as well be a bank teller, right? Or sell insurance or drill teeth or something. I like a job with a little challenge to it."

"You want to watch the door while I go through the files?"

"You expecting somebody?"

"Maybe. I got a feeling." But I wasn't and I didn't. I just said that to cheer Booker up, to give sentry duty a little edge so he wouldn't feel he'd wasted his time.

I went straight to Jack's files and looked up Koehler. Then I looked up the names of all the other clients in the stolen file. Then I looked through Jack's desk and on top of it and all around the office.

The upshot was, whether I liked it or not, I had to give Blick credit for good instincts. The Koehler file was missing and none of the others were.

So it looked like someone connected with the case had killed Jack, stolen the Koehler file to cover his tracks, and then stolen my dupes of it as soon as he found out I was working with Jack. There just wasn't any getting around it.

"Okay, Booker," I said. "Let's go."

"Find what you wanted?"

"Yeah."

"Well, where is it?"

"In here," I said, tapping my temple.

"Christ, you're leaving empty-handed?"

"I wanted information, my boy. You don't need a pillowcase to carry that off."

"Shit," he said, and picked up an orange plastic ashtray on Jack's desk. He stuck it in his pocket. "It's not official till you steal something."

"Booker, I need another favor."

"It better be more exciting."

"It'll probably hurt your professional pride."

He sighed. "Okay. Shoot."

"Could we go out in the hall and break in again? This time with a credit card?"

"Hey, man, I've got the best key collection in six counties. You want a Visa artist, get an amateur."

"Just this once?"

He sighed again. "Come on."

We went out in the hall and closed the door. Booker produced his loid and let us back in, approximately five seconds from the moment the lock went click. It might not have been his greatest accomplishment, but it impressed hell out of me.

I forgot to be nervous. "Show me how."

He did. It took a few minutes and a few tries, but I got it down. Easiest thing in the world and kind of thrilling. I began thinking maybe your mother didn't have to be gay to produce a burgling son, and put it out of my head right away. I was too poor and vulnerable to be fantasizing a life of crime—the thing seemed entirely too possible.

I dropped Booker at his chic Russian Hill digs and tried not to think about how he paid for them. Then I tried to think of something I could do besides go home, because if I did that, I would probably be forced to think about the shambles my life was in, there being no TV on the premises. But I couldn't go anywhere because I didn't know anybody who'd want to see me and I didn't feel I could afford a movie. A bottle of jug wine would be slightly cheaper and have longer lasting anaesthetic effects.

So I ended up at home again with Mondavi Barberone. I couldn't tell if the sun was over the yardarm, since I didn't have the least idea what a yardarm was, and anyway, the fog was in; so I took a wild guess, decided it was, and poured myself a glass of purple pleasure. Then I sat down to survey the damage.

I strode bravely into the cobwebby corners of my psyche and I rooted around. There was some very ugly stuff in there, and it is a mark of my spiritual growth that I currently have the nerve to put it down for anybody to read.

These were the facts: I was thirty-eight. I'd spent fifteen years on one major metropolitan daily or another. I'd written six unpublished detective novels. Unpublished in spite of my name.

John D. MacDonald did it daily. Ross Macdonald did it deeper. Gregory Mcdonald did it with dash.

Wrote thrillers and got them published.

But not Paul McDonald.

I just wrote them, supporting my habit with clients like Jack.

Pretty soon, I figured, some publisher was going to see the light. It had to happen—it was inscribed somewhere, like the Second Coming, I figured. But meanwhile, I was thirty-eight and putting on a brave face for people like Debbie Hofer.

Debbie and a lot of my ex-colleagues thought I was a model of courage to quit the *Chronicle* and suffer for my art. They were pretty amused when I talked about being a ghostwriter for a private eye.

But they didn't know what it was like in those

25

cobwebby corners. I had a nice line of patter that made them think I was Joe Carefree, just a rake and ramblin' man.

Women liked it, too; I was a big hit on the first date. But usually there wasn't a whole lot more dates. You don't have a lot to say to strangers when what you do all day is fill up blank sheets of paper with imaginary sex and violence. You could talk about your disappointment and desperation, but they wouldn't want to hear it.

So I was a lonesome cowboy. Spot's company needed supplementing.

It was getting to the point that my mother was asking not-so-subtle questions aimed at determining whether Sonny was gay or not.

I wasn't, but I knew it was pretty rare for a guy my age to be a bachelor. Unmarried middle-aged women aren't so rare, and neither are divorced men—even twice divorced at my age. But I didn't know any other guys who'd made it this far without so much as living with someone for more than a few months—which I hadn't—and I was starting to wonder why and whether I was ever going to find a woman.

I hated thinking about that kind of stuff, but I'd made up my mind to root around in the corners and I figured I might as well do it right.

And that meant I couldn't ignore the fact that I didn't have anything to offer anyone anyway. I owned one minuscule bit of real estate and a cat and a car and a stereo, but I couldn't even afford a secondhand TV to replace my stolen one.

Not that I wanted the kind of woman who was looking for a sugar daddy, but I did want one who was going somewhere in the world, and a woman like that wouldn't want me. Because I wasn't.

I had about two hundred bucks to last me the rest of my life.

My only client was dead.

The market for mysteries was terrible.

I didn't get out enough.

I was getting crotchety.

The only thing I'd ever done successfully was write newspaper stories.

And I was sitting on a great story.

I picked up the phone and dialed the *Chronicle*.

CHAPTER 4

I asked for Joey Bernstein, who's the city editor and the sweetest guy in the world.

"McDonald, you nerd. I'm on deadline."

"I've got to talk to you, Joey."

"The only thing I want to talk to you about is when you're coming back."

"I don't see why you're so sore about my leaving—you've got fifty or sixty other reporters."

"Yeah, and most of them a lot better than you are. It wasn't the fact that you quit, shithead; it was the way you did it."

How I did it was, I sent him one of my favorite records—"Take This Job and Shove It" by Johnny Paycheck. I thought he'd be amused.

"Joey, I apologize. I thought you liked country music."

"Are you coming back to work or not?"

"How about temporary?"

"Okay. Nolte's going on six months' leave."

"I had in mind about two weeks."

"McDonald, give me a break. What good's that going to do me?"

"I meant two weeks' special assignment. I've got a fantastic story, Joey, my boy. I mean, fantastic. You know Jack Birnbaum, the P.I. that got poisoned?"

"Yes."

"Well, have you noticed that Lindsay Hearne is mysteriously on leave from 'Bay Currents'? What if I told you those two things are connected?"

"You would have my full and complete attention."

"Lindsay's married to Jacob Koehler, first of all."

"The gene-splicer."

"Right. Here's how it shakes down: Lindsay met Jacob on an interview ten years or so ago when she was a humble newspaper reporter. They got married and their union was blessed with issue. But they made like atoms when little Terry was five. At first they had joint custody, but then Jacob remarried and Lindsay relinquished her half of Terry, the better to pursue greatness, I guess."

"Get to the point, McDonald."

"Well, Lindsay had Terry every other weekend, and thereon hangs our tale."

"She snatched her."

"Right you are. About three weeks ago. And Jacob hired Jack Birnbaum to find the kid."

"Hang on a minute. The station must know where she is."

"Uh-uh. She phoned in sick the Monday after Terry disappeared, but apparently not from home—could have been from anywhere. And then she resigned formally in a letter which her producer received the following Wednesday, posted Saturday from San Francisco."

"So if she's quit, why are they saying she's on leave?"

"They want her back. She has a contract and they don't

want to let her out of it without a fight. Anyway, that's not the point. The point is, Birnbaum was killed because of this case."

"How do you know?"

I ran it down for him, about the files and all. He was suitably impressed. "So what are you going to do if I put you on the payroll? Solve it?"

"Right, chief."

He sighed. "Be careful, Paul."

He hung up before I could ask to be switched to the library. So I called back and broke the news that I was back, however briefly. Then I named a few names and pretty soon a female voice was reading to me. It was very soothing.

The voice read me a story written about Lindsay Hearne four or five years back, when she won the Peabody Award, which, I gather, is something like a Pulitzer in the broadcasting field. Lindsay won it for exposing a massive cover-up involving a breeder reactor at a government lab in the East Bay Hills—a machine that was masquerading as some sort of helpful friend to mankind, but which could be used to whip up a little plutonium any time a bomb was needed. She got that story when she'd been in San Francisco about six months.

Before she came here with Koehler, she'd been, as I told Joey, a humble newspaper reporter. She'd worked first in Louisiana and then in Michigan. She hadn't won a Pulitzer, but that was about the only journalistic honor she hadn't bagged before she went into TV, which was an excellent move on her part.

She was a great reporter. I said it and I meant it. Great. One of the best I ever saw. And she was also a fine figger of a woman. TV was unquestionably her medium.

After the soothing voice got done with Lindsay, I asked it to move on to Jacob. It said Jacob had worked at Stanford with Paul Berg, the first guy to get the Nobel for genetic engineering, which, in case you don't know, is a simple little process by which you can recombine DNA, the stuff that genes are made of, and invent new organisms. You probably think only God can make a tree, and you're right; scientists just splice viruses and bacteria together to make new bugs. But gene-splicing is thought to have quite a future.

Anyway, Berg did it first and he was Jacob's mentor. Then Jacob improved on Berg's method and won his own Nobel.

Other whiz kids in the field, Herbert Boyer and Ronald Cape, left their respective universities and founded genetic engineering companies, Genentech and Cetus. But Koehler and Stanley Cohen, another protegé of Berg's, stayed on at Stanford.

That is, Koehler did until the fall of 1980, when he and his brother Steve founded Kogene Systems.

They went into business just about the time Genentech, then four years old, offered its stock on Wall Street. You remember that. The offering price was $35 a share and within a few minutes it went up to $89. Brokerage houses ended up having to ration the stock. And Genentech didn't even have a product on the market.

The voice read me a little yarn about the formation of Kogene Systems, which said Steve had ponied up the money for it.

So I asked for the clips on Steve Koehler.

Steve sounded like a man for the ages—or at least the decades. In the seventies, he made money in microcomputers, which were about as high tech as you could get at the time. In the eighties, he'd apparently cashed in his chip money and put it on the come line. I liked his style.

I thanked the nice librarian and rang off. It was just after five o'clock by that time, but who knew how late geniuses worked? I called Jacob Koehler at Kogene Systems.

A female voice answered and I very distinctly asked for

Jacob, but somehow I got Steve. What the hell, I needed to see him, too; so I told him what I wanted—or rather I didn't, exactly, on the theory that I didn't yet know either of the brothers well enough to broach the subject of whether one of them had killed Jack.

"This is Charlie Haas at the *Wall Street Journal*," I taradiddled. "We'd like to do profiles on you and your brother for a little story on genetic engineering."

"I see. You're doing a general story on the whole field?"

"Actually, we're sort of concentrating on Kogene. The newest of the highest tech—state of the art and its future. That sort of thing."

"A science story?"

"Mostly a business story, really."

"I see." He seemed to perk up a little. "When would you like to meet?"

"How about tomorrow morning?"

"Eleven o'clock?"

"Great. Could I see both of you at the same time?"

"I'm afraid it'll just be me. When we started Kogene, we decided I would be spokesman for the company."

"That's fine. You can speak for the company. All we want from your brother is a personality profile. He's a pretty well-known guy, after all. It wouldn't look right to do a whole story on Kogene and not have a word from its principal asset."

"I'm afraid he won't agree to it, Mr. Haas. It's not really his policy to talk to the press."

"Okay. We can talk about it tomorrow."

I guessed Jacob had good reason to be allergic to interviews—he'd gotten a bad marriage out of one once.

CHAPTER 5

Kogene is out by Cetus in Emeryville, a weird little town tucked in a corner between Berkeley and Oakland. Emeryville has a population of something like 4500, a little over half of whom live in sauna-infested condo complexes. That half tends to be white and well-off. The other 2000, who tend to be poor and parti-colored, live in tiny houses on tiny streets surrounded by windowless industrial caverns that hover nastily. Cetus sprawls through several of the caverns; Kogene is squeezed into one. A small one.

Someone had made a genuine effort to class up the reception area, which was all white and plant-filled. But no one had soundproofed it; I heard voices from somewhere in the recesses as soon as I crossed the threshold.

"We've got to get another one. I've got to have her back." A male voice, upset. Then footsteps; someone walking even deeper into the recesses.

"Is anything wrong? With Lindsay?" A female voice, slightly alarmed.

"No, no, of course not. The cleaning lady just quit, that's all." A different male voice, reassuring. "Have you got enough material?"

"Sure. I'll call you later in the week." The female voice again, and then a female—presumably its owner—stepped into the reception room.

She was tall, but not too tall, and thin but not skinny. She had soft, regular features, except for a square jaw; thick, shiny light brown hair; great legs. She looked like a nice girl from a good family. She just missed looking like a WASP princess ex-cheerleader post-deb preppy powder puff, and the reason she did was that she looked smart. Something about her bones or the line of her cheek was her saving grace—I couldn't tell just what, exactly. But I could tell she was not only no dummy but also somebody who was going somewhere in the world. I thought of asking if I could go with her, but I lost my voice for a moment there.

"Mr. Haas? Mr. Koehler is expecting you."

What do you know? There was a receptionist there. The ace investigative reporter hadn't even noticed.

Steve Koehler came out to meet me, which, I felt, showed a reasonable amount of class. He had an Ivy League accent, nice manners, and the uniform that went with them—gray flannel slacks, blue blazer, and cranberry tie. A walking cliché.

He was a tall dude, and skinny, kind of gaunt around the cheeks like a serious runner, but slightly soft around the middle like he wasn't so serious. I figured he was about my age, but he had less hair, and what he had was dark and vaguely curly. His eyes were sort of filbert-colored and the only interesting thing about him so far.

Women probably liked them, but I didn't. They belied the impression of substance he'd cultivated so carefully.

Back in the recesses, he sat me down and gave me coffee.

"Sorry my brother can't make it. He said to give you his apologies."

"Let's start with you, then. I take it you run the business."

"Yes."

"What's your background?"

"Oh, Harvard Business School, a little time in the family business back in Chicago, and then Silicon Valley. I got lucky. I met up with a couple of computer wizards who were working out of their garage at the time, got into silicon chips, and made enough money to help Jacob start Kogene."

"What's the family business?"

"Real estate."

"Are you married?"

"Divorced."

"Age?"

"Forty-one."

"Where do you live?"

"San Francisco. Telegraph Hill."

"And your brother?"

"My brother?"

"Where does he live?"

"We don't usually give out that information. The truth is, Mr. Haas, my brother is something of a recluse. You know how these geniuses are—wrapped up in their work and not very sociable."

"He's lucky to have you to fend people off."

Steve didn't answer. Just gave me a filbert-eyed stare. I looked at my notebook. "Let's see. Did I ask if you have any scars or other distinguishing marks?"

He let a corner of his lip turn up, just to be polite. The result was a fourth cousin to a smile.

"Nobody ever likes these preliminaries, but we have to

have little facts to go between commas. You know, like 'Steve Koehler, forty-one, a native of Chicago.' Which reminds me—how old is your brother?"

"Forty-three."

"Okay, let's talk about Kogene a bit. You mentioned that you made enough money to help Jacob found it—was that a long-standing dream of his?"

"Not exactly, no. Scientists don't really think in terms of making money. They just do research, and when they're done doing it, they do more research."

"So the company was your idea?"

"Primarily, yes. But Jacob is very happy with it, of course. He has more freedom this way."

"How many employees do you have?"

"About fifty, I think." Fifty! Genentech had several hundred and it was a lot smaller than Cetus.

"You see, Mr. Haas, we've deliberately kept ourselves small. At the moment we are primarily a research firm, and our research is very specific."

"Oh?"

Again the smile-cousin. "We hope to have a product on the market within a couple of years. A very, very important product."

I'd read that some gene-splicer or other had already whipped up bacterial insulin, and there were a few other offerings in the health field, as well as schemes to invent new plants that would fertilize themselves and maybe grow in salt water. But the potential product with the most razzle-dazzle was biosynthetic interferon, a protein that might or might not cure cancer, and maybe the common cold and herpes as well. If anyone could make it do any of those things, he'd have a very important product indeed. But every scientist in the field was trying to do that. Surely if that's what the Koehlers were on to, Steve would have said so. Just in case, I gave him another chance.

"Interferon?"

This time he smiled a real smile. I'd said something that made him happy. "No. Oh, we're working with it— everyone is—but the product I mean is something else. Unfortunately, I'm afraid I'm not currently at liberty to tell you what it is. I can tell you, though, that we'll be making an announcement in the very near future. We also plan to make a public stock offering soon."

"How soon?"

"Within about three months, I should say. Possibly in September."

"And how much stock will you offer?"

"Something in the neighborhood of $250 million."

I almost said, "You gotta be kidding," but I remembered my manners in time. I didn't say anything.

"Does that surprise you, Mr. Haas?"

"I can't say that it doesn't. Cetus offered about half that when they were ten years old and already had several products to sell."

"Our stock is going to be worth a great deal more than theirs."

"Forgive me if I ask you why you say that."

"Of course. And I'd like nothing more than to tell you, but the time isn't right."

"Why all the mystery?"

"We're just not ready to make the announcement, that's all. If you've finished your coffee, maybe you'd like to look around the plant."

"Sure."

He picked up the phone and gave orders. "Young John Reid will show you around," he said. "I don't know much about gene-splicing myself—he'll explain it much better than I could."

"Do I have to wear a lab coat or anything?"

Koehler laughed. "Nobody else does. In fact, why don't

you leave your coat here? You're a bit overdressed for Kogene."

I shed it gratefully. I had a sweater underneath and the day was getting warm.

In a moment John Reid appeared. He looked about twenty-five, wore faded jeans, and had the build of a tennis player—in other words, nothing like my idea of a scientist. As we went through what Koehler called the "plant," I was forced to revise my stereotype—the scientists were all like Reid, except for the women, who had breasts.

Their labs were decorated with photos of their most recent camping trips and each lab blared a different rock and roll station, except for one that went in for country and western.

The equipment wasn't impressive at all, even the thing called the gene machine. The place looked as if it could have been on a college campus.

"Do you understand what we do here?" asked Reid.

"Well, I . . . uh . . ."

"Let me start at the beginning. The thing we splice into bacterial DNA is a human gene. The new organism can then make a protein that may become a drug. That's what it's all about."

I nodded. I hadn't a clue that was the way it worked. But Reid had a way of explaining everything so simply that I almost caught on to a lot of it.

First he showed me the organic synthesis lab, where the gene machine was making synthetic DNA. "Linkers" made this way can be used to hook a gene to a plasmid, which can then be put into bacteria. Once you've got your new bug, you "grow it up" in vast fermenters in other labs. After you grow it up, you have to harvest it, or "take it down." That means getting rid of the growing medium so that what you have left is "cell paste," which you have to keep refrigerated at −80 Celsius.

Somewhere in your cell paste is your product, but the problem is, it's still in the cells. So next you have your "purification" step, in which you must break open the cells and separate the protein of interest from all the others in the cell, and there could be a couple of thousand of them.

I think that's the gist of what Reid said. He was very patient.

I saw the labs where all those things were done, but nowhere did I see Jacob Koehler. "Nobody goes in his lab," said Reid. He pointed to a closed door. "Just Jacob and his wife. And sometimes his kid."

"His kid?"

"Yeah. Terry. She's supposed to be super-smart or something."

"You mean she *works* in that lab?"

Reid shrugged. "That's what her dad says. Maybe he's putting the rest of us on."

That sounded right to me.

When the tour was over, my head hurt. I needed a new super-absorbency brain—the one I had just wasn't getting the job done. Reid took me, limping—mentally, anyway—back to Steve Koehler.

I donned my coat and sat down for a post-tour chat. It seemed to be what Koehler had in mind, too. "How long," he asked, "have you been at the *Journal*, Mr. Haas?"

"I'm not actually at the *Journal*. I just free-lance for them occasionally. Which brings me to something else I meant to ask you. I was thinking of doing a piece on your brother and Lindsay Hearne for *People*. Fun-couple sort of yarn. You've probably noticed those things are pretty short and sweet. Think he'd agree to that kind of interview?"

"Hardly. They've been divorced for two years. Jacob's married to Marilyn Markham now—our second most distinguished biochemist."

"Oh. I didn't realize. But that might even be better—two scientists working side by side, creating new life

41

forms together. Sort of romantic, don't you think? We could get a picture of both of them in their white coats, recombining away."

"I'm sure Jacob would never agree to it." He extended his hand. "If there's anything else I can do for you, let me know."

I said I would. Then I stopped in the lobby for a moment and spoke to the receptionist, casual-like. "Could you tell me something? I'm just curious. That lady who came out when I came in—wasn't that Nancy Allen? You know, the actress in *Dressed to Kill*?"

She smiled—a real smile, not a fourth cousin. "Sort of looks like her, doesn't she?"

I did what I hoped was a fair imitation of a man whose face has fallen. "You mean it wasn't?"

"Nope. That was Miss Kincannon of Pandorf Associates. Some sort of artist, I think."

"Sardis Kincannon?"

"Why, yes, I believe so." She checked an appointment calendar. "That's right."

It wasn't the kind of name you forget, and I'd heard it before.

Jacob Koehler had given Birnbaum a list of Lindsay's friends to check out. He'd gotten to all of them except one. Sardis Kincannon.

CHAPTER 6

This was great. Here was a lady I wanted to meet and now I had an excuse. Maybe my luck was changing.

If she worked for Pandorf Associates, that meant she was probably a graphic designer; or maybe she was some sort of C.I. executive. Once I did a story on advertising, and I knew all about C.I. It meant corporate identity. That was something a high-priced firm like Pandorf could create for your firm for several hundred thousand dollars. Or you could pick a designer out of the yellow pages and have a logo done for about $500. As far as I could see, C.I. and logos were about the same.

Probably Miss Kincannon was whipping up a new corporate identity for Kogene now that the company had big plans. Probably Steve Koehler had recognized the importance of presenting an exciting new face to the public. The importance of that and a fat tax deduction.

If I could find out from Miss Kincannon what sort of

identity the corporation was getting, maybe that would help me figure out what the mystery product was. It could be important, especially if I ever had any money to invest.

Anyway, maybe she knew where Lindsay Hearne was. Jack hadn't asked her because she was out of town when he was in the asking business.

Furthermore, I could use a corporate identity myself. It never occurred to me before, but suddenly I myself recognized the importance.

That made three reasons to call her. So I dug in my pockets for one of my last dimes. "Miss Kincannon? My name's Paul McDonald and . . ."

"Who?"

"Paul McDonald. I'd like to talk to you about doing my corporate identity. Steve Koehler recommended you."

"Oh. But . . ."

There was a long silence as she apparently reconsidered whatever it was she was about to say.

I seized the advantage. "Would you like to have lunch? I mean, if you haven't already."

"Uh, well . . . I was just going out. Are you in the neighborhood?"

"I am, yes. I'll be right there." And I hung up before she had a chance to think about it.

I wasn't anywhere near the neighborhood. I wasn't even on the right side of the bay. But my old Toyota was not only fast, but cunning. I figured I could be there in fifteen minutes if I didn't have parking problems.

Needless to say, Pandorf Associates had put quite a bit of thought into its own corporate identity. From what I knew about the firm I figured it thought it was young, chic, hot, expensive, dynamic, going places, on top of things, sophisticated, cosmopolitan, glamorous, and at the same time a bit unconventional, eccentric even, as befits the artistic temperament. No doubt that's why it had its

44

executive offices aboard an old ferry. The whole damn office was moored on the Embarcadero.

I made it in twenty minutes, but that wasn't quick enough for Miss Kincannon. She was in the boat's reception area, which was all cozy and gold and brown. There was even a wood stove in case you missed the point.

Miss Kincannon was wearing her coat and gnawing on her fingernails. I could tell by the look on her face that they weren't satisfying her and that she was only seconds away from starting in on the furniture. She had two very serious-looking lines on her forehead, right between the peepers. I knew these signs—the nail-gnawing, the unsatisfied look, the lines. These were the signs of a woman who would soon be biting your bicep if you didn't get a sandwich inside her instantly.

I panicked. Sinbad's, which was where I'd planned to take her, would probably be crowded. I was trying so hard to think of another place that I forgot to introduce myself.

"Mr. McDonald?"

"Oh. Hi. Yes."

"I remember you. You were at Kogene this morning."

"I remember you, too. You didn't look quite so hungry at the time."

"I am *faint* from hunger. *Weak*." She had very little southern accent, but she used the sort of dramatic intonation I associate with Dixie belles. I hoped it only came out under stress.

"We've got to do something about your blood-sugar level. Do you have to have food right away or will a drink do it?"

"I'd *love* a drink."

Good. If there was a crowd at Sinbad's, we could wait at the bar and my bicep would probably be safe. But there wasn't a crowd. It was nearly two o'clock, and that was probably why. It also accounted for Miss Kincannon's faintness and weakness.

45

We got a table outside, right on the water, practically under the Bay Bridge, with Treasure Island nearly at arm's length. It was gorgeous, and so was Sardis Kincannon in my book, even with those two funny lines in her forehead.

They smoothed out after about half a glass of white wine.

"So, Miss Kincannon"—what a suave devil I am— "what part of the South are you from?"

"For heaven's sake, call me Sardis. This *is* California, isn't it?"

"Yes, and very few of its residents bear the name of the ancient Lydian capital. You have to go south to find much of that."

"Well, I am from the South; it's true. But I'm not named after any old ancient city." She'd dropped the italics; thank God.

"There's another Sardis?"

"Yep. A reservoir in north Mississippi. I was conceived on its shores, in the back seat of a car."

"Mississippi! I knew it."

"What about you, Paul? What kind of corporation are we identifying?"

"Well, now, if I had you people do my corporate identity, what would I get? I mean, a logo and what else?"

She laughed. "People always think it's just logos. C.I.'s a lot more than logos."

"Well . . . like what?"

"It's how your corporation projects itself to its various publics—your employees, your stockholders, your clients, and the general public are your four publics. We like to call C.I. an identity system that visually separates and distinguishes a firm from its competitors." She was warming to her subject, slipping into her own corporate identity. Her voice was getting crisp, and to my mind, a little phony. She was starting to sell. People always get earnest when they're selling something and I don't like them as well. She

46

was no exception, but it was my fault she was on the subject and I'd just have to take the selling side of her.

I interrupted her. "But what could I get? Business cards and stationery, right?"

"On our corporate identification checklist, we have nineteen classifications under stationery alone. Then there's your literature—your annual reports, quarterly reports, brochures, catalogs, newsletters, and what-have-you. All that's got to be designed. Then there's transportation: your trucks, company aircraft, all that—even your parking lot decal. People forget about things like that. After that, there's your packaging, your architecture, signage, marketing and sales material, employee relations designs, dining accessories, operational materials. To name a few."

"What, pray tell, is an 'employee relations design'?"

"Well, let's see—how about a five-year pin?"

"You people don't miss a trick, do you?"

"A lot of people seem to feel they need our services." She was getting huffy, but I didn't care. I thought this stuff was garbage, and as you know, I'm not very emotionally mature. I did not exercise the self-control and tact the situation called for.

"Need it for what?" I said.

"Look, do you know what a corporate image is?"

"Isn't that what we've just been talking about?"

"No, indeed. Your corporate image is the way your company feels it projects itself to its publics. Your corporate identity is the actual impression it's making. You follow that?"

I nodded.

"So the extent to which the two things are disparate is the extent to which you need me. Or would, if a small-time detective agency had any publics to impress."

For a while there, I was pretty bored and busy with my crab salad. But that last sentence got my attention. I was so

47

surprised, I blurted the first thing that came into my head: "I'm not a detective."

"You aren't?" She blushed, seeing several hundred thousand Pandorf dollars go down the tube.

I shook my head.

"There was just a story in the *Examiner* about a guy with your name . . . for some reason I thought . . ." She was stammering. She'd been damned sure I was the Paul McDonald in Ben McGonagil's story, which meant she'd taken careful note of the name. It also meant she'd been leading me down the garden path for the last half hour— she knew as well as I did that I wasn't going to buy any high-priced C.I. But what the hell? The whole point of this lunch was to get some questions answered, and now I was spared the trouble of exposing my own fraud.

I gave her a break: "I am that guy. But I'm a writer, not a detective. In fact, at the moment I'm a reporter. I'm working on a story about Birnbaum's death."

I filled her in on the ghosting and my current job at the *Chronicle*. She was understandably confused.

"But what do you want from me?"

I told her about the Koehler case. Or I started to, anyway. She got big tears in her eyes almost as soon as I mentioned Lindsay's name, and they started running down her face when I said she was missing.

"That's what Jacob meant. This morning."

"Jacob?"

"Jacob Koehler. He came into Steve's office, looking all wild-haired, and said something about how he had to have her back."

"I think I heard it. Was it just as you were leaving?" She nodded. "As I recall, he said, 'I've got to get another one.'"

"Another private eye he must have meant."

"He sounded pretty distraught."

"Jacob's crazy. Always has been." She dabbed at her eyes.

"Still, he must have recommended you for the job. The C.I. for Kogene, I mean."

"He did. I've been working on it for months. And this morning he acted like he never saw me before in his life. Cuckoo."

"The original absentminded genius."

She nodded. "I don't know what Lindsay saw in him, except looks, maybe. Glamour." She'd stopped crying now and she put away her hankie. It dawned on her that we were off the subject as she knew it. "Wait a minute. I thought you wanted to talk about Birnbaum."

"Did you know him?"

"No. When I got back from vacation, there was a message that he'd called a few times. "That's how I knew the name."

"He was contacting all of Lindsay's friends."

She didn't speak, but she looked inquisitive as hell.

"Sardis, I'm afraid Lindsay's disappearance and Birnbaum's murder are connected." I told her about the burglaries.

"I see," she said. "But what can I do for you?"

"I want to know what you can tell me about Lindsay. How do you know her?"

"We were best friends in college. Still are, I guess. Except . . ." The tears started again. "Oh, God, I feel awful. She's had problems and I . . ."

I waited.

" . . . I guess I wasn't there for her. I was too busy with my own problems."

"What sort of problems? Lindsay's, I mean?"

"I don't know. I honestly don't know. That's why I feel so awful. All I know is that she's been terribly depressed the last—oh, three months or so. Maybe more. I mean,

49

she was depressed the last time I saw her, and that was two months ago."

"How often did you see her?"

"Once a week, usually. Once every two weeks at the least. I just . . . didn't call her for a while. I didn't realize it was such a long while."

"She didn't call you, either."

"She probably didn't feel like it. I wasn't very good company at the time. She probably couldn't stand to be around me. All I ever talked about was my own problems."

"Did she say what she was depressed about?"

"No. She wouldn't talk about it. But I probably didn't give her a chance."

"What sort of person is she, Sardis?"

"The sort who always knows where she's going. When we were at Sophie Newcombe, even. She was editing the school paper and doing a campus radio show while everyone else was trying to set new world's records for gin-and-tonic consumption. I admired her a lot because she never let things get her down. The South, I mean. New Orleans. Sororities and fraternities. I had trouble . . . relating, I think it's called now."

"Misfit, huh?"

She looked at me gratefully. "I never could figure out what anybody or anything was all about till I came to San Francisco."

"And Lindsay?"

"She was too smart for the kind of garbage everybody else was handing out down there, but she just didn't let it bother her. She used it for her own benefit, somehow. Pretended to fit in even when she didn't. Didn't get in arguments about race or religion. Just swam with the tide. Wish I could have done it."

"Did you ever think it was odd that Jacob had custody of Terry?"

50

"Uh-uh. If you ask me, Lindsay just wasn't cut out for motherhood. She struggled along with that joint custody till Jacob remarried, but he didn't exactly have to twist her arm to get her to see it his way after that. Terry just kind of cramped her style. It was Jacob who wanted kids in the first place."

"Are Terry and Jacob very close?"

"Oh, yes. She's a prodigy, you know—supposed to be as smart as he is."

"A young scientist at Kogene told me he used to have her work in his lab with him. But I didn't put much stock in it. I mean, a seven-year-old . . ."

Sardis nodded. "It's true. I don't know how much she really understood—all I know is that Jacob claimed she was on her way to becoming a scientist. He had her in there a lot."

"Oh, lord. I'll bet she's a horrible little brat."

"Not really, no. A little strong-willed, but pretty well-adjusted, for a genius."

"If Lindsay didn't want her in the first place, and then had problems with her, don't you think it's pretty strange that she snatched her?"

She considered. "Come to think of it, yes. I'd have to say it's an un-Lindsay type of thing to do. It interferes with her career and her social life, and it's impetuous. Or seems impetuous, anyway. Definitely not like Lindsay. It's scary."

I knew what she meant, but I didn't say anything.

"I mean, maybe she didn't snatch her. Maybe she's in some kind of trouble."

I avoided her eyes.

"She could be dead, couldn't she, Paul?"

I didn't answer.

"Do the police know about this?"

"Well . . . no. And I'd appreciate it if you didn't tell them."

"Why?"

I couldn't tell her I was having a childish feud with Howard Blick. In fact, I couldn't think of one good reason why she shouldn't tell them. "I have my reasons," I said. I sounded dumb even to myself.

"What reasons?"

"Uh, it might endanger Lindsay's . . . uh . . ." There were big hunks of time between the words; any fool could tell my heart wasn't in it, but I was committed and so I was going through with it.

Sardis got up and towered over me. "Endanger your precious story, you mean. No wonder you worked for Birnbaum. You're as low-down as he was."

This took me by surprise. But I handled it intelligently. "Huh?" I said.

"Why don't you ask me about A&L?"

I would have, but she got up and left before I could. It wouldn't even be unreasonable to say she stalked out, if you go in for that kind of colorful phrasing.

Now what the hell was A&L? And why did she think Birnbaum was low-down if she didn't know him? And why did she agree to have lunch with me if she knew I didn't want my C.I. done?

These were a few of the questions I turned over in my head while I paid the check and waited for my change. I also wondered what else she knew about this case and whether she knew where to find Lindsay. She didn't, I thought—otherwise, she wouldn't have been talking police with so much enthusiasm.

Police. I thought about them all the way home. Once again I tried to think of one good reason not to call them and tell them what I knew. Then I tried to think of a half-baked reason. I didn't complete either mission.

At this point, I really was impeding a murder investigation. Blick had been right about the motive for the murder and I had confirmed that he was right in an effort to prove him wrong and I was currently just being a bad sport.

I was going to have to swallow my pride and tell him. I resigned myself to it and vowed to do it instantly, the second I got home. Oh, what a good boy was I.

As usual, I parked on Chenery Street across from my house. I admired my paint job, locked the Toyota, and started across the street absently, just performing a familiar act I performed two or three times a day.

I could have admired my own paint all the way across the street, as I sometimes do, but that particular day I decided to compare my house with the Hathwells', two doors down, which hadn't been painted in years. I had to look slightly to my left to do that, and that's how I happened to notice that a car was coming right at me, quite a bit faster than a speeding bullet.

CHAPTER 7

Reflex is a wonderful thing, full of surprises and revelations. If you'd told me I was going to be in a situation like that, I have no idea what I'd have told you I'd do, but here's what I did do: I jumped straight up in the air and leaned backwards.

I came down very hard and painfully on the pavement, and I rolled back towards my car, but the rolling was superfluous—the other car was long gone. I didn't get the license number.

I did get about three thousand bruises. Blick had his counterrevenge for my last revenge, although he didn't know it; I figured if I'd told him about the missing files yesterday, he'd have solved the case by now and this would never have happened. Can you imagine having that much faith in Blick? It gives you some indication of my mental state. I was feeling not only hurt and defeated but also disoriented, because I was pretty well terrified.

There was a stop sign at my corner, so that car couldn't

have been driven by some random rocket jockey who didn't see me. It had to have pulled out of a parking place someplace behind me, where its driver was waiting. It didn't stop to see if I was hurt, and it didn't try to swerve to avoid me. So its driver was trying to kill me. That was the only conclusion you could draw from the incident, and that's why I was pretty well terrified. I figured if he tried once, he'd probably try again. And next time he might have better luck.

I dialed Blick, said I had some important information for him and asked if he could come over. He said sure.

While I waited for him, I tried to put things together. Why would anyone want to kill me? I was kind of an easygoing guy, more sinned against than sinning, even in matters of the heart, I felt. So revenge was out.

I was currently not involved in any triangle whatsoever, so jealousy was out.

No one stood to inherit from me, either.

Of course the thing had to do with the Birnbaum case, and I knew it. I was just fooling around before I got down to serious thinking about it.

The murderer had stolen my copy of the case reports after reading about me in the *Examiner* and now he must be trying to kill me because I knew what was in the reports. I took time out to shudder, imagining what might have happened if I'd been home when he came for the reports. Then I got back to business.

Okay. So I knew too much. But what the hell did I know? Those case reports were completely innocuous, so far as I could see; even a little on the slender side. A lot on the slender side, come to think of it.

Jack was a funny guy to work for. On some cases, it seemed like he detected his buns off, and I was impressed as hell. On others, it seemed like he hardly did anything to justify his two hundred bucks a day, and I was hard put to make him look like a hero on paper.

Such a case was the Koehler one. I even asked Jack about it; he said that nobody understood how much background checking a detective had to do, that they took it for granted you just went out and asked a few questions and people answered them just like that. He groused about it so much I figured I'd hit a sensitive spot and shut accordingly up. But there was hardly anything in those reports.

As I recalled, Jacob had given Jack just five names to check out. I made a list of them: Sardis Kincannon, Joan Hearne, Susanna Flores, and Mr. and Mrs. Timothy A. Hearne.

The Timothy A. Hearnes were Lindsay's parents, who lived in Atlanta, and the first report I'd done for Jack described in detail how he'd hired Atlanta operatives to watch the house, how they had indeed watched the house, how they had contrived little tricks like posing as this or that repairman to get in the house, and how they could report with certainty that neither Lindsay nor little Terry was there.

Joan Hearne was Lindsay's sister, age thirty-three, and a vice president of the Women's Bank of the Golden State. Not the biggest bank in the Golden State, but an up-and-coming one. The Hearne sisters seemed to be a motivated crew.

Joan told Jack that Lindsay called her the Saturday morning she disappeared and said she was about to make the snatch. But according to Joan, she refused to say where she'd be on grounds that it was safer that way. It sounded pretty unlikely to me, but Jack said he believed her. All the same, my report went on, Jack was monitoring her mail in case Lindsay wrote. That may or may not have been illegal, assuming all he did was look at the postmarks, but it was unquestionably ineffective. Lindsay could write to Joan at the bank, or at a post office box, or at a neighbor's, for one thing. But most likely she'd phone. So what was the point of mail-monitoring?

To misguide the client into believing he was getting his money's worth, so far as I could see.

Anyway, Joan provided one other pertinent bit of information, dutifully recorded in one of our reports: She said Lindsay had a boyfriend, a guy named Peter Tillman.

That fact inspired Jack to do some of his famous "background checking" on Tillman before gumshoeing off to question him. He found out the guy was forty-two, a wealthy real estate developer, and married.

Tillman was understandably reluctant to talk to him. But he did say he'd had a date with Lindsay for Friday, the night before she disappeared, and that she broke it, saying she was sick.

Susanna Flores, the final person on the list, was Lindsay's producer. She was the one who provided the information about Lindsay calling in sick, apparently after mailing a letter that said she was actually resigning. She was very close to Lindsay and pretty shocked by her behavior. Shock must have made her lower her guard, because she asked Jack if he'd talked to Michael Brissette, Lindsay's ex-boyfriend. Jack said no, but he would.

And he did. I presume he didn't need to do much "background checking" on Brissette, since he was a household word—a San Francisco supervisor with plans to be the next mayor.

Brissette, a lawyer by trade, said he hadn't heard from Lindsay in months, until the Wednesday before she disappeared. That night, he said, she called him on a legal matter. He wouldn't tell Jack what it was.

That sounded promising, come to think of it. But it was about the only thing in any of the reports that did.

I thought about typing all that stuff up and maybe giving it to Blick, but there wasn't really any point in it—

he could just get the originals from Jacob. Anyway, he was already ringing my doorbell.

"This better be good."

"Someone just tried to kill me."

"Couldn't have been a jealous husband, McDonald. You're not the type."

Now, was he saying I wasn't the type because my ethics were exemplary, or was he taking another shot at my bearlike physique? It was a way he had, putting a person off balance.

"Somebody tried to run me down. I mean it."

"Now who'd want to kill you?"

"The same person who killed Jack Birnbaum, maybe." I swallowed hard. "You were right, Howard," I said. It hurt, but not as much as I thought it would. "I think he was killed by someone connected with the case we were working on."

"And who might that be?"

"Christ, Howard, how would I know? You're the detective."

"You don't know who killed Birnbaum, but you now think the motive had something to do with the case that you used to think was too routine even to consider."

"That's right."

"So what made you change your mind, asshole?"

He wasn't making it easy. I decided to give him a little of his own. "Someone stole the goddam file," I said, "in case you didn't notice."

I could see his face twitch a little—he really hadn't thought of that. "You got any proof?"

"Yes, I have proof, goddammit! A San Francisco police inspector with a search warrant tore my entire house apart and didn't find it!"

"Maybe you flushed it down the toilet, McDonald."

"Howard, for Christ's sake. I'm trying to cooperate."

59

"Why would he steal your file, McDonald? He'd have to steal Birnbaum's as well."

"Why don't you check it out?"

"I will. What's the client's name?"

"Koehler. Jacob Koehler." I spelled it for him.

"So what was the case?"

"Ask him."

"I'm asking you."

"Why don't you ask me about how somebody tried to kill me?"

"You know why, McDonald? Because I don't give a shit, that's why."

He left without saying good-bye.

I figured this round was mine. He got to be nasty about whether my life was at stake, but he was so mad he forgot to ask for Koehler's address. That meant he was going to go to Jack's office, look for the file, and fail to find it. Then he was going to have to call me to find out how to find Koehler. And that would be a conversation I could have some fun with.

I did type up my notes on the case. It gave me something to do while I was waiting for Blick to call. It occurred to me that one of the folks I was setting down facts about was a murderer, maybe. Probably not the Timothy A. Hearnes, and almost certainly not Sardis, since she'd been away during the whole snatch, investigation, murder, and everything. It might be one of the other four and it might not. All it had to be was someone who knew about the investigation, which let in Jacob and probably his wife, and probably Steve Koehler and who knew how many other people at Kogene. Swell.

The phone rang.

"McDonald? Who's this Jacob Koehler, anyway?" It was Blick.

"You mean you don't know?"

"How the hell would I know?"

"I thought everybody did, that's all."

"Goddammit, McDonald, who is he?"

"Why don't you look him up in Birnbaum's files?"

"I did, dammit. He's not there."

"Oh." I let a little time pass, waiting for him to ask me again. He did.

"Who is he, dammit?"

"He's a Nobel laureate, Howard. Just about the hottest scientist in the country."

"Oh. Well, how do I get hold of him?"

"That's your problem, Howard."

I hung up, feeling the score was getting pretty close to even. My conscience was clear, because anybody, even Blick, could track down one of the hottest scientists in the country. But I could have saved him a few phone calls, which I had failed to do, and I had also had the pleasure of making him admit his ignorance.

So much for revenge. Now I had to work on the case. I mean, the story. I was getting carried away with this detective business.

Blick would be getting to Jacob pretty soon, and Jacob would turn over the one remaining copy of the reports, and Blick would start hitting the people on the list. I already knew who they were, so I could get to them before he did. Brissette was far and away the most promising.

I changed into a sports jacket and tie, fed Spot, and drove to City Hall. I went into the supervisors' collective office, across from the second-floor pressroom, and asked to see Brissette.

His administrative aide was named Janet, a plain, pleasant girl I knew from my days with the *Chronicle*. She said he'd just stepped out, probably to the men's room.

"Mind if I wait?"

"Of course not." She showed me into his cubicle.

I waited fifteen minutes, maybe, and Brissette didn't turn up.

61

A million things could happen to a supervisor on the way to the men's room—he could run into loquacious old pals or pleading supplicants. Or angry constituents, or nosy newsmen. Any of these would slow his progress.

Or he might drop into the second-floor pressroom for a chat, or pop down to the cigar stand for a candy bar. He could even duck into a phone booth and call his girlfriend. But Brissette was divorced, so he wouldn't need privacy for that. Well, he could call one of those ladies who talk dirty and put their fee on your credit card. I didn't have anything to read, so I just let the possibilities run through my head.

But since I have a short attention span, pretty soon I started thinking about how to improve the quality of my waiting life. I could go buy a magazine, but that would cost a buck and a half or so. I could walk across the hall to the pressroom and renew old acquaintances, but that would be depressing. It might remind me that I might have to apply for a permanent job in a pressroom if things didn't get better.

Kathy Wong wasn't depressing, though. She covered the courts for the *Examiner* and she worked out of a different pressroom—the one on the fourth floor. She kind of had a way of lifting a person's spirits just by being alive. I wondered if she was dating anybody. And then I remembered that I was currently employed by her competition, which meant I couldn't tell her my troubles even if I could lure her out for a drink. So much for Miss Wong.

On the other hand, the fourth-floor pressroom was the one broadcast people worked out of on the rare occasions that they graced City Hall with their august presences. Reporting sullied their images, so they didn't do too much of it. But maybe some of them would be there today, and maybe I could pick up some gossip about Lindsay Hearne. Or better yet, Susanna Flores.

I told Janet I'd be back in a minute, and I left.

I could have taken the elevator, but I never had when I was working in the second-floor pressroom, and I didn't see why I should start now. Or I could have taken one of the big, stately staircases. But I'd never done that, either.

City Hall also has some hidden staircases—not hidden, really, because all you have to do to find them is open a door that says Stairs—but most people don't notice them. Even City Hall employees don't use them much. But I always had, partly, I think, because they were so often deserted. It was eerie being completely alone in such a public place, and I got a kick out of it.

I wasn't looking for kicks that day. I just took those stairs out of habit. Or almost took them, as it turned out. I didn't get very far.

There was a man sprawled out on them, between the second and third floors. It was Brissette.

I galloped the few steps up to where he was lying and stooped. He was very still and there was blood coming out of his mouth. I felt for a pulse, as I had with Jack, and had a strange sense of déjà vu. Once again, I felt helpless—I didn't know if someone was dead and I didn't know what to do for him if he wasn't.

I raced back over to the supervisors' offices and cornered the clerk.

Without a word, he followed me back out the door and up the stairs.

Other people from the office heard me, and they followed too, also silently.

"I think we'll need an ambulance," I said to no one in particular, and one or two people turned back, to call one, I suppose, or simply to avoid looking at Brissette.

The clerk and I got him off the stairs and onto the lower landing. One of the women loosened his tie.

When we put Brissette on the landing, I took off my coat, wadded it up, and slipped it under his head. And when I did that, I touched something disconcerting—

63

something around the back of the head that felt soft when it ought to have felt hard. Suddenly I had to find a men's room.

When I realized I wasn't going to make it, I remembered the sink in a sort of utility closet at the back of the second-floor pressroom. I barged in, raced through the room, and threw up all over the day's crop of dirty coffee cups.

Pete Lufburrow, my ex-colleague from the *Chronicle*, stopped typing and hollered: "McDonald, I thought I told you never to eat in the City Hall cafeteria."

I staggered into the pressroom proper and said: "Mike Brissette fell down the inside stairs."

Three chairs squeaked on the old tiles as the three reporters in the room rose in unison, grabbing their notebooks. "Dead?" asked Lufburrow.

"I don't know."

I could practically feel the breeze as the three whizzed out of the room. Naturally, Lufburrow thought this was his story since City Hall was his turf, and so far as he knew, I didn't even work for the *Chronicle*. But I had a prickly feeling it was going to be my story before my two weeks' employment were up. I called Joey Bernstein.

"McDonald, you gotta start keeping in better touch. I've got something for you."

"Joey, for heaven's sake, I've only been out-of-pocket for about forty-five minutes and meanwhile I got you your lead story for tomorrow."

"Bullshit! The lead story's—" Then he caught on. "What's going on, Paul?"

"I'm at City Hall. Mike Brissette's badly hurt."

"Holy Christ!"

"Lufburrow's on it, but listen, he doesn't know a couple of things I know that you ought to know."

"Like what?"

"His head's caved in in the back. It looks like he fell

down the stairs, but I have a feeling he might have been sapped."

"And why, pray tell?"

"I'm no expert, but I don't see how you could get that kind of injury just falling down. That's one thing. But there's another—he's connected with the Birnbaum case."

"Holy Christ!"

I filled him in on the details.

"You're a good boy, Paul. Come back to work for us, okay?"

"I am working for you, Joey. Hey, I found him, didn't I?"

"Did you?"

"I guess I forgot to tell you. I'm everywhere at once, kid. I've got my finger on the pulse."

"I've got bad news for you."

"Yeah?"

"When you called in, I thought I could make you real happy. I had a page 1 story for you. So now you've called in an injured supervisor, but it's Lufburrow's story. So see what you just did, Mr. Finger-on-the-pulse?"

I sighed. "Knocked my own story off page 1."

"You got *too* good a nose for news, pal."

"What's my story, anyhow?"

"Koehler's decided to go public on the kidnapping."

CHAPTER 8

It seems Jacob Koehler, the eccentric who never gave interviews, had simply picked up the phone, dialed the *Chronicle*, and said he had a story. He was switched to the city desk line that such calls go to—known to the staff as the nut line—and was engaged in the uphill work of trying to explain to some jaded copyboy that he really was a Nobel laureate who really was divorced from a television personality when Joey walked by, caught the name Koehler, and took the call.

Joey made us an appointment for 5:30 P.M. at Koehler's Emeryville condo—it seems the Koehlers were among the well-heeled white folks who lived in the good part of town, with all the saunas and pools.

They lived in the oldest of the condo developments—a place called the Watergate. You can look it up if you don't believe me.

I didn't have much time before the appointment, but

there were a couple of things I wanted to clear up before I left City Hall.

Outside the pressroom there was bedlam. The news had spread, and everyone was in the corridors, on the rotunda stairs, all over—they were watching Brissette being carried out on a stretcher. Lights and wires were already all over the place, signifying the TV folks had swung into action.

I went back to the supervisors' office and looked for Janet: I figured one of Brissette's colleagues would have gone to the hospital with him, thereby hogging a little publicity, and Janet would have been left to answer phones.

The phones were already ringing, but the place was deserted. I went back outside.

And there she was, fighting her way up the rotunda steps, harangued and bullied by my brethren in the broadcast media. She was crying so hard she was tripping over their wires.

But in case I haven't mentioned it, journalism is a dirty job. Even though any fool could see now was not the time to bother her, I was about to do it, too. I'd had years of practice at being the kind of asshole a reporter on deadline is, and I hadn't forgotten how. I went back to Brissette's cubicle. I knew she'd fight off those turkeys in a few minutes and then go there to repair makeup, call her boyfriend, smoke a joint, or whatever she did to relieve tension.

She jumped when she opened the door and then, recognition dawning, fell into my arms, sobbing and holding on like she was drowning and I was a passing inner tube.

Comforting ladies, unlike being an asshole, was not something at which I was practiced. I improvised. I patted and soothed and every now and then said, "There, there," or something.

Pretty soon she calmed down a little and I got her some water.

"I'm sorry, Janet," I said. "I don't know what to say."

"Thanks, Paul. Thanks for being here. I mean, I guess you're here because you want to know something, but I'm glad it was somebody nice."

I felt like a jerk, but I had a dirty little job to do and I did it. "I wanted to ask you," I said, "if Brissette left the office to meet somebody."

She looked surprised. "No. I mean, I don't think so. He just left without saying anything, as if he were stepping out to the men's room."

"Did he get a phone call before he left?"

"Well, sure. Lots. Supervisors get so many phone calls you don't notice."

"Do you screen them?"

"No. Why?"

"I just wondered. I was also wondering something else. Was he in the habit of using the inside stairs?"

Again she looked surprised. Very surprised. "Not that I know of, no. I wonder why he took them today?"

She started to cry again, thinking, no doubt, of the cruel irony of it all.

"I'll leave you alone," I said. "Stiff upper lip, kid." And I gave her hand a little squeeze. I was getting sort of good at soft stuff.

I went back to the pressroom. By then everyone had finished calling in his story and the gang was sitting around having a postmortem gossip.

"How's Brissette?" I said.

"McDonald, goddammit, you get back there and clean up that mess in the sink."

"I—uh—forgot." And I'd have liked to go on forgetting, but with six angry eyes upon me there wasn't much choice. I got back there and cleaned.

And while I cleaned, I listened.

69

"While they're putting his head back together, maybe they'll make him a new nose," Lufburrow said.

I heard laughter, but apparently not everyone joined in. "I don't get it," someone said.

"He's got no nostrils left. Well-known fact." The speaker was a crusty old dude who worked for the *Examiner*.

"If he ran for mayor, I'd think twice before I contributed to the campaign," said Lufburrow. "He'd probably snort up all the contributions."

Everybody laughed again.

So Brissette was a cocaine freak. Who'd have thought it? It didn't fit with his Mr. Moderate image.

I finished up and came out in the pressroom again. "How's Brissette?" I said again.

Lufburrow shrugged. "Who knows? It'll be a while—always is."

"You didn't happen to see what happened to my jacket, did you? I put it under his head."

"Oh, yeah. Janet said it was yours. I brought it up." He gestured towards his cubbyhole-office, and I went in and plucked my coat from the rack. A bit wrinkled, but good enough for a scientist.

I told the boys good-bye and hit the road.

On the way to Koehler's I couldn't help thinking about Brissette, despite my best efforts at repression. I was wondering if he'd been hit and if it was my fault. Maybe if I hadn't played that little game with Blick, he'd have gotten to him earlier and Brissette would have unloaded what he knew and Blick would have had enough sense to figure out what it meant and the murderer would have been safely under arrest and Brissette wouldn't have got hit. It was a sobering thought. I hated it. I can't tell you how much I hated it. Because if there was the dimmest possibility in the world that it was true, I was going to have to do some serious thinking of the type I hated worst in the world. I was going to have to root around in corners of my mind with Do Not Disturb signs on them—musty alcoves I hadn't visited for twenty, maybe thirty years, and never wanted to see again.

Something like that, in abbreviated version, went through my head when I felt that soft spot on Brissette's. That was why I puked.

The Watergate was much like a condo complex I knew in San Francisco, which was very similar to another I'd been to in San Mateo. I think the same guy designed them all, and maybe lots of others as well. He didn't seem to go in much for modifications.

Marilyn Markham let me in. She was short and dark. A bit overweight perhaps, but sensuous, with large breasts under a navy sweater. Her features were heavy and her hair was the hair of a woman who couldn't be bothered getting it cut right. Or I suspect that's how she looked at it, but it was my experience that women who didn't bother with their appearance were afraid to. I don't know if they were afraid they still wouldn't look good or if they were afraid they would.

Marilyn wasn't the beauty Lindsay was, but she was a lot of woman. I could feel it, just standing in the doorway. She was someone to be reckoned with, someone to push against—a strong-willed, determined someone who was probably squishy like a rubber duckie when little Terry. All that and a first-rate scientifi catch, Jacob.

"Come in, Mr. McDonald," she said. " at the moment."

I came in. Jacob was sitting on a forlorn as it's possible to look when three, with the kind of shoulders yo every day.

He stood up to shake hands, a

length of him. He was wearing tan corduroy trousers and a blue collared sweatshirt. He had a slender, powerful body topped by those massive shoulders and a fine, craggy-featured head with slate-blue eyes in it. On the head was a curly mop of gorgeous gray hair. It was a joke, he was so handsome.

As a pair, he and Lindsay must have drawn crowds.

He motioned me to sit down and sat himself. "I felt this interview was absolutely necessary," he said at last. "Desperately urgent."

I caught a motion of some kind out of the corner of my eye and, turning, saw that Marilyn had either signaled him or given an involuntary jerk of some sort. She seemed very upset.

"But now," said Koehler, "I don't know. Marilyn—I mean, we've had some rather upsetting news."

"We've been burglarized," said Marilyn.

There was a lot of that going around.

"It isn't that so much," said Jacob. "The burglary was Tuesday, actually. We're upset because the police seem to feel it may be connected with this . . . terrible thing." Jacob got big tears in his eyes. "Her own family," he said, "her own flesh and blood. I don't see how she could . . ."

Marilyn went over to him and took his hands. She whispered something I couldn't hear.

"I already know something about this," I said. "I was assisting Jack Birnbaum on your case."

Apparently not everybody reads the *Examiner*. Koehler ooked amazed; I continued. "I wasn't working for the *nicle* at the time. I was helping Jack prepare case for his clients. And right after he died, someone my house and stole my copies of the reports we

didn't seem to be taking it in.

ndering," I finished, "if that's what

Koehler looked almost grateful that he wasn't going to have to start from square one explaining the thing. "I think it is, yes. An Inspector Blick called on me at the lab today. Do you know the inspector?"

I said I did.

"He told me that Birnbaum's death might be associated . . . somehow associated with me. With my problem." He looked completely bewildered, very much the genius without a soupçon of common sense. "He asked for the reports, so I brought him home to get them and . . . they simply weren't here. I'd put them on my desk—just on top, under a paperweight. I called Marilyn, and she hadn't seen them."

He looked at her, as if for confirmation. She nodded.

"Then the inspector asked if we'd noticed anything odd, anything misplaced, as if someone had broken in, and I remembered we were burglarized. We came home and some of Marilyn's things were scattered around. They took a few pieces of jewelry. That was all. I mean, we thought that was all."

"That's what mine was like," I said. "They took my TV to make it look as if that's what they were after. I didn't discover the files were missing till the next day."

"What my husband's trying to tell you, Mr. McDonald," said Marilyn, "is that we've decided not to seek any publicity about the kidnapping."

"I wanted to make a plea," said Koehler, "for any information about Lindsay or Terry." His voice dropped when he mentioned Terry, the way some people's drop when they mention their favorite deity. "But now this thing seems so serious. So complicated. We just—Marilyn and I—don't think it's the right time to do it."

He looked at Marilyn for approval. She looked at me. She smiled. "We're sorry, Mr. McDonald."

I could have pushed the thing, but I didn't. It wasn't the story I was after, and if it didn't run, there was less chance

73

of tripping all over Ben McGonagil on the way to the biggie. So I didn't ask for any more explanations.

"I'm sorry, too," I said. "And please let me know if you change your mind."

They said they would and I left, feeling a bit bewildered. Why hadn't they called and canceled, I wondered? Either they were very rude and insensitive folks or they had made the decision at the last minute. I inclined toward the latter theory.

But why? If they wanted to make a plea before, why not now? I didn't see how the bad news could have made a whit of difference as to whether it would be appropriate.

I just didn't get it.

I stopped at Denny's, the closest fast-food joint to the Watergate, and ordered a burger. The decor was monochrome (mustard-colored plastic), the clientele polychrome. Most of the men wore short-sleeved shirts, a sure sign of working-class status. Apparently this was a popular spot with the folks from the wrong side of town.

While I waited for my order, I phoned the office. First I said there wasn't going to be a Koehler story and then I asked about Brissette. He was dead on arrival at Central Emergency.

It was what I expected, but somehow I didn't expect to take it so badly. I went up to my neck in the Slough of Despond the second the receiver clicked back into place. I knew I couldn't eat my burger, and I should have canceled it, but I couldn't get the words out. I didn't want to talk to anyone.

So I just left. I got in my Toyota and drove back across the bay, toward San Francisco. That was where I lived, but I didn't want to go home. There was no one but Spot there.

As soon as I thought that, I could see the paradox in it. I didn't want to talk to anybody, but I didn't want to be alone. That certainly simplified matters.

74

The thing to do, I supposed, was go to a bar. That way I could have as much human contact as I wanted and never have to say a word to a soul.

But it probably wouldn't work that way. I'd go in all morose, and I'd drink something or maybe a couple of somethings, and then things would start looking better. I'd perk up a little and someone would get up the nerve to speak to me, and it would be a dumb someone with nothing interesting to say. And I'd talk to him—or her— because I didn't want to add any more layers of jerkhood to my already severely endangered soul.

I looked at my watch. It was early yet. Barely 6:30. Maybe I could find someone to have dinner with, someone I wouldn't mind talking to. But who?

It was a dumb question. There was only one person I wanted to have dinner with and she didn't like me. Ordinarily I wouldn't have called someone who didn't like me, but this was an emergency. I went home and dialed Pandorf Associates. She was still there.

"Hey, listen," I said. "I'm really not as low-down as Birnbaum. It only seems that way until you get to know me. Underneath the hostile asshole most people see, there's a sweet, timid guy struggling to get out."

She did me the honor of a polite chuckle. "I was snippy. I'm sorry."

"You mean the hatchet's buried? Just like that?"

"Sure."

"I can't believe it."

"Why not?"

"I thought I was going to have to plead with you over dinner. I mean, that was going to be my excuse for asking you to dinner. Now I don't have one."

"I . . ."

I talked fast, not letting her get a word in. "Some guys would give up at this point. But not me. No sirree. I'm

75

going to think of another excuse before you have a chance to turn me down. Just watch. I'm thinking now."

"Listen, Paul, I . . ."

"I know. We've gotta celebrate. That's it."

"Celebrate what?"

"Resolving our differences. It's a momentous moment."

"You're sweet, but really, I have a lot of work to do. Maybe another time."

"Sardis? I really need somebody to talk to." It was hard for me to say stuff like that, but I felt pretty strongly about seeing her.

"You do?" she said. "About Lindsay and all that?"

"Yes. Would you have dinner with me, please? I could have you back at your office in a couple of hours."

"Oh, the hell with it. I'll come in early tomorrow."

We went to Basta Pasta, which is one of two restaurants in town that always seem to feed you even if you don't have reservations.

A little red wine, a little French bread, and both of us started to unwind. For a while we just kind of chatted, like any couple on a first date. She was a curious young woman—twenty-eight years old and still angry about a lot of things. It was hard on her, being an adolescent misfit; it was hard on all of us, but she was in the South at the time and she said that made it worse.

She'd come to California with a degree in art and a lot of talent and chutzpah (to hear her tell it, anyway), and she'd started out doing paste up for a firm of graphic designers. For the first time in her life she met the kind of people she always imagined there must be somewhere, and these people she described as the sort who would speak to her honestly without meaning something other than what they were saying.

About then I started catching on that maybe her adolescence actually had been tougher than the average.

Anyway, she later moved to another firm, where she

was a designer herself, and from there to Pandorf, where she was an executive—a "project coordinator," meaning a person who organized the getting together of C.I.'s. She'd been doing this for two years and she was beginning to hate it. She wanted to paint.

Much like a thousand other stories in the naked city. Much like mine, when you got down to it. But I found her fascinating. She seemed a lot like me in a lot of respects—her background, all that early teenage, early young adult stuff, and her anger, held even after it was all over and she had come out on top. I identified with it as if I were in her skin. I carried the same anger and I knew it.

But that wasn't what made her fascinating. It was the way she was different from me. She had a softness, a vulnerability, a way of speech and manner that seemed to treat each person she met—me, the waiter, each fellow human being—with a respect that bordered on awe. How could she be like that and be so much like me? That was the fascinating part.

After she told her tale, I reciprocated with a little spellbinding information about myself—how I was the first person in my family to go to college and how I had to clean toilets to do it, even though I had scholarships, and how I became an ace but unappreciated reporter for a metropolitan daily and ultimately a ghostwriter for a private detective.

I even mentioned Maureen to her, and I didn't talk about Maureen much. She's kind of the one who got away, though I doubt if she'd see it that way. I said something to Sardis that I'd never said before. I said that I regretted losing Maureen. The reason I never said it is that I never thought it before. Never thought it because I was the one who dumped Maureen.

Lately, though, something funny had been going on. I'd started feeling things I hadn't felt before, and one of them was Maureen-regret. It probably had to do with my age and level of achievement. I wished it would get lost.

Anyway, the thing about Maureen popped out and all of a sudden Sardis was crying. I didn't know what to say. I offered her some water and she refused. Then I just sat there, twisting my napkin till she could speak.

"I'm sorry," she said. "I'm feeling sort of vulnerable."

"You regret something, too," I said.

"Yes. But he dumped me, you see. I couldn't stop the thing."

"Was it recently?"

"Last month."

"I'm sorry."

"I want to tell you about it. I think you ought to know."

I didn't really want to know, to tell you the truth. I hardly knew this woman and the *ought* in her sentence sounded possessive. It sounded like maybe she thought we were going to be seeing each other on a regular basis. That got my hackles up.

Why? you may ask. You might point out that I thought she was terrific in just about every way and she was the only person in the world I wanted to be with that night. So why didn't I like the idea of seeing her on a regular basis? Well, I did, so long as she wasn't so amenable to it. Does that make sense? Hell, no, of course it doesn't.

But that's the way it was. I didn't like Sardis thinking there was somethng I ought to know and I didn't want to hear her goddam heartbreak story. I didn't want to hear anybody's heartbreak story; I didn't want to know anybody that well.

But I couldn't ask her not to tell it without alienating her forever, and if I did that, I couldn't see her on a regular basis. See what a bind I was in?

I answered her as noncommittally as possible. "Oh?" I said.

"I just had an abortion. I mean, a few weeks ago." Her eyes were filling up again.

"That's tough," I said, hoping I was making my voice gentle enough to sound sympathetic. God, I was awful at this stuff. I was embarrassed as hell and beginning to sweat.

"The man I was seeing was married and he lied and . . . it's the usual story."

I nodded. I knew exactly the story she meant.

"The thing was, the guy was a client. He stopped using Pandorf when it was over. I mean, he stopped on account of me. I personally cost the company several hundred thousand dollars."

Maybe I didn't know what story she meant. Maybe I was losing my grip. Was her heart broken, or was she worried about losing business?

"I shouldn't have gone out with a client. It's unprofessional as hell, and I could probably get fired for it. But probably I wouldn't get fired. Probably I just wouldn't get any good assignments anymore. It wouldn't happen to a man, of course, if the situation were reversed, but that's the breaks. It's happened before at Pandorf, and at other corporations I know of. Your career just sort of unofficially stops dead. You get a 'reputation,' like in the nineteenth century."

"But if no one knows about it . . ."

"Jack Birnbaum did. I thought you ought to know."

Oho. "I thought you didn't know him."

"Those messages he left. The first two said he wanted to talk to me about A&L. That's the name of my friend's company. The third one mentioned the man by name. So that's how I happened to remember your name after I saw it in the paper—I was pretty interested in the Birnbaum story. And that's why I spoke to you sharply at lunch. I'm sorry."

I took her hand. I didn't know what to say again.

"What the fuck," I said at last, "was Jack up to?"

"I thought you might know."

"Let's have some more wine. It might help us think."

We did, and it did. But not right away. This is the way with wine.

We kicked the thing around awhile.

Finally, it occurred to me to ask an obvious question. "What did you think when you saw the messages?"

"I got sort of paranoid about them."

"What do you mean?"

She looked embarrassed. "It's dumb, but for some reason I got the idea of a blackmailer in my head. I mean, I know it doesn't happen much in real life, especially when you haven't got a lot of money in the first place, but it popped into my head." She shrugged, as if to excuse herself.

"Maybe that's not so crazy." My mind was humming along like a Japanese import. "Maybe Jack had a habit of buying information. I mean, maybe he was going to use Mr. A&L as leverage with you—to make sure you told him what you knew about Lindsay."

"My God. You'd work for a man like that?"

"I didn't know. I mean, I don't know. But I never liked the guy much, if you want to know the truth. I guess I thought he was a little sleazy." It was my turn to shrug. "I sort of thought it went with the territory. P.I.'s have had a pretty bad reputation ever since Philip Marlowe went out of action."

"Nonsense. Marlowe lives."

Sardis was nothing if not full of surprises. We'd have to explore the subject of Chandler in depth. But some other time. My little brain was still busy.

"There was something about Jack that always struck me as peculiar. Sometimes reasonably easy cases seemed to take a lot longer than they ought. He explained it by saying he had a lot of 'background checking' to do. So take this as a hypothesis—he investigated everyone he wanted to question before he questioned him, only going to the questionee when he finally had something damaging on him. Something to use as a persuader. Does that fly?"

"It's weird. If he was going to be a blackmailer, why not blackmail people for money instead of information?"

"Maybe he did both. Maybe that's what got him killed."

"Omigod. Do you know who else he talked to about Lindsay?"

"Yes. Why?"

"Was Mike Brissette one of them?"

I saw what she meant. There was a guy with something to lose. And he'd been as blackmailable as a movie star with a rap sheet. He had a coke habit a twelve-year-old could ferret out. But I didn't think he killed Jack.

"You know Brissette?"

"Not really. Lindsay talked about him, that's all."

"He was killed this afternoon. I found the body." I picked up my wineglass and drained it. The time had come to alter my blood chemistry. For a while I'd been pretty successful forgetting things I wanted to forget, but now I had to think about them.

"Killed! Was he murdered?"

"I don't know. I think he may have been." I told her the story. And then I told her about the attempt on my life. I got drunker and drunker as I did it.

I hated the whole situation. I hated having someone on the loose who wanted to kill me and I hated possibly being an unwitting instrument of Brissette's death and I hated needing somebody to talk to.

In the morning I'd probably hate myself for getting drunk and forever ruining my chances with Sardis. But getting drunk I was.

I'm pretty good at disguising it, though, so she didn't catch on right away. Not only did she consent to let me drive her home, but she invited me in and offered me a brandy. I had three. Four, maybe.

By then I had the courage to make a pass at her. We were sitting on her sofa, at opposite ends. I was thinking she had the greatest legs I ever saw. On the pretext of putting my glass on the coffee table, I moved a little closer to her. Then, very suavely, I put my right hand on her left breast and squeezed.

She yelped.

Not only that, she leaped up. Terrified, maybe. Repelled more likely.

"Paul McDonald," she said, "you are definitely not driving home." And she disappeared.

When she came back with a pillow and blanket, I was already half asleep. She leaned down to tuck me in and I grabbed her right breast. What a sophisticate.

No wonder I was so popular.

CHAPTER 9

I was right about one thing. I hated myself the next morning. I had such a hangover that losing my chance with Sardis seemed secondary. I woke up way the hell early, a frequent occurrence when I've overdone. Some people say you wake up like that when the alcohol has left your bloodstream, but I don't believe it. If it's not there anymore, why do you feel so lousy?

Sardis was still asleep and I didn't want to wake her, so I didn't even scrounge around for coffee. I just left, thinking I'd call her later at Pandorf and thank her or apologize or something.

It was maybe 7:30 when I turned onto Chenery Street. Already light. But my house didn't look quite right to me. It was strange because other people's looked the same as ever.

When I got closer and saw what was wrong, I couldn't take it in. Bad news is like that.

But a long time has passed since then and I have come to believe it happened, so I can now write down with perfect confidence what it was: Sometime in the night my house was gutted by fire.

I got out of my car and the air smelled funny. That was further evidence that it was true. But I still didn't believe it, so I walked to the front door and looked in. I wished I hadn't. It was like looking at the body of a dead friend; nothing like the live person had been. It wasn't a house at all anymore—just a stucco shell with black streaks all over its nice terra-cotta paint.

Somewhere in the rubble, I supposed, there might be something that could be salvaged. I'd have to look, eventually. But Spot's body would probably be in there, too, and that was literally the body of a dead friend. I didn't want to find it. At least I hadn't lost my life's work—I'd stashed copies of all my manuscripts, including my current one, at Debbie Hofer's, just in case.

At the end of the front walk there was a little step, and I sat down on it, feeling about as bereft as it's possible to feel, I guess. Maybe it hurts more to lose a wife or kid, but if your house and cat are all you have, they become more precious than they'd be to a guy with a wife and kid. Because you know how close you are to having nothing. And that's what I currently had.

I was going to miss Spot.

For a long time I sat on my step feeling numb and awful. A couple of people came out to get their papers and I was afraid someone would speak to me; I didn't want to talk to anyone, so after a while I got in my car. My throat felt tight and every muscle in my face was straining. My body wanted to cry, but it couldn't. Crying wasn't a skill it had learned.

My next door neighbor came out to get her paper. Her name was Mrs. Civkulis. She saw me, waved, and started walking toward the Toyota. I pretended not to see her. I liked her, but I couldn't face her then. She started hollering my name. I left her in a cloud of dust.

Where to go, though?

The Toyota answered me. It turned toward North Beach and headed there without my help. North Beach was where Sardis lived. Once again, when I thought I didn't want to talk to someone, it turned out I did. This was getting to be a habit.

She was just leaving for work. Already outside, turning her key in the lock.

"Paul!" She seemed glad to see me. Can you feature that? Then she saw what I looked like and she closed up her smile. "What happened?"

"My house burned down."

"Oh, no," she said, or "Oh, shit." Whatever people say when they hear someone else's bad news. The thing she said wasn't memorable. The thing she did was. She walked over to me and kissed me all over my face, saying between pecks how sorry she was.

No one had ever done anything like that for me before. Maybe I hadn't ever been as vulnerable as I was at 8:30 that morning.

She led me into her apartment and put on some water for coffee. Then she called her office and said she wouldn't be in. She was putting herself way out for a perfect stranger. I didn't know what to make of it.

I seemed to be slow getting the hang of anything that morning. I guess I was in shock.

Sardis poached eggs and made toast. "Are you insured?" she asked.

Of course I was. I hadn't even thought of it. I was about to come into a lot of money. So why wasn't I happy?

A nod was all I could manage.

She sat down and took my hand. "You'll be okay, Paul. There are other houses."

I nodded again. But I was starting to feel the least bit

hopeful. Something about the way she spoke—the tone of her voice or something—made me feel as if I *might* be okay.

"There's something I'm afraid to ask," she said. Her face was very solemn. "About Spot."

"How do you know about Spot?"

"You talked about him last night."

"Oh, shit."

"It was sweet, actually."

"I didn't see him," I said.

"Oh." She waited.

"I didn't look for him."

"I'll do it," she said. "You don't have to come."

"No," I said. I was confused and embarrassed. She seemed to have grasped the situation, and that confused me. I thought people thought I was tough and hard. But she didn't. She knew how much I cared about a damned cat and I wasn't sure I wanted anyone to know, including myself. It was embarrassing. So I didn't say the right thing.

"Paul," she said very gently, "he might be okay."

"I didn't mean no, you shouldn't look. I meant I'll go with you. It just didn't come out right."

She stood up and kissed me on the forehead. "My car or yours?"

"Mine, I think. Driving'll give me something to do."

It did. At least it kept me from biting off my fingernails. But it failed to fill up the old brainpan. The shock was wearing off and I was starting to wonder about something. The something was how the hell a decently wired, unoccupied house with no glowing embers lurking in its crannies happened to catch fire on a quiet night in a quiet neighborhood like Glen Park. I had a feeling the answer was going to be spectacularly unreassuring.

Sardis sucked in her breath when she saw the house, but

she didn't say anything. She couldn't control her face, though. She looked so unhappy that this time I kissed her. I kissed her and then I shrugged and let my eyebrows go up. That was my usual mannerism when I was upset and trying not to show it.

Sardis asked if she should go in alone and I shook my head. I didn't want to go worth a damn, but I thought I should.

We got out and marched up to the door and opened it. It felt the way it feels when you first get off the plane in Mexico in the winter—so hot it's hard to breathe. Funny, I hadn't even noticed the heat earlier that morning. Sardis gasped, maybe at the heat, maybe at the decor, which was early charcoal briquet. I felt sick again. Neither of us went in.

"Spot?" said Sardis. "Here, kitty, kitty, kitty."

Her voice was a little weak, but she sounded almost normal. Here was an ordinary, beautiful, nice lady calling a cat just like any nice lady might, only she was standing in the doorway of a burnt-out shell of a house in which not even a cockroach could survive and the cat wasn't going to come and it was my cat. Despair hit me like an avalanche.

"He's not there," I said gruffly, sounding not nice at all. I started to step away from Sardis, but she stepped away instead.

Maybe Sardis was shocked; maybe she even got teary: I didn't know. Right then I didn't give two sticks of gum for her or anybody else. What I had to do was protect my ass. Moments like that—when you feel shitty and another person can see it—can get you into the kind of trouble I didn't want to be in. You might start feeling something for that person and that's dangerous as hell.

"I shouldn't have brought you here," I said. "Let's get the hell away." From the sound of my voice you'd have thought I was talking to somebody trying to mug me.

I didn't even look at Sardis. I just turned and walked toward the Toyota. Mrs. Civkulis, damn her, chose that moment to come out and express her sympathy. At least I assumed that was on her mind, and I didn't need her goddamned sympathy.

"Mr. McDonald," she chirped. "Oh, Mr. McDonald." She was walking fast and waving her hand at me. The sound of her goddam cheery voice made me want to puke.

She caught up with me halfway down the walk and put her hands on me. Actually grabbed me by the arm. I shook her off and kept walking, not even looking in her direction. I got in the Toyota and hollered, "Sardis, come on, goddammit!"

But Sardis didn't. She went over and talked to Mrs. Civkulis, apologizing for me, no doubt. It made me mad as hell. So I started up the Toyota and drove away. I just left the bitch, that's all. I figured she could find her own damn way home. I didn't need her in my life and she could get the fuck out of it.

I left the bitch, all right, but I didn't have anywhere to go. That dawned on me after two or three blocks. I started feeling bad again. Another two or three blocks and I felt awful. Also guilty as hell and thoroughly ashamed of myself.

About half a mile later I started facing facts—I had to go back and get her. She'd been terrific to me and I'd been an asshole to her and she'd probably never speak to me again, but at least I had to offer to take her home. If she spit in my face, as she damn well ought to, I could just go home as usual and brood about yet another failure with yet another woman.

Only I couldn't. I didn't have any home.

That's what I was thinking when I drove up in front of my house-shell, and I was feeling mighty low.

But I experienced what the shrinks call a sudden mood swing when I saw what was on the step—Sardis with a big fat smile on her face and a large cardboard box beside her. The box had holes in it. It said Porta-Pet on its side.

Summoning forgotten reserves of mathematical genius, I put two and two together. I jumped out of the car; Sardis jumped into my arms and I picked her up and swung her around, just like guys do in the movies.

I don't think I'd ever been that happy. There's something about hitting rock bottom that makes two inches higher seem like Mount Diablo. I'd still lost my house and my typewriter and my blue-green sofa, but by God I had my cat. And Sardis not only didn't hate me but actually seemed a little bit fond of me. I felt like a goddam zillionaire.

It was scary, though, because I still hadn't sold a book. Would it feel this good? Was I ever going to feel this good again? I started worrying almost immediately and that got me a little less happy, which was a more natural feeling. I relaxed a little.

I went over and spoke to Spot, and he answered me in Cat-speak. Then I spoke to Sardis: "I suppose I ought to go and thank Mrs. Civkulis."

She shrugged. "You could call her later—I think she understands that you aren't exactly feeling sociable this morning. Anyway, she didn't have to enter any burning buildings to save Spot. He came to her door and asked to be let in."

I spoke to the box. "Good thinking, Spot-o."

Sardis spoke to both of us: "Do you guys have a place to stay?"

We didn't, and that was the truth. There might have been this old buddy or that old pal or maybe Debbie Hofer wouldn't mind, but there wasn't what you'd call an obvious choice. I was mulling that over when Sardis spoke again: "You can sleep on my couch if you like."

"No, thanks. I can—"

"Stop being a jerk." She was angry, and that got me angry.

Why would you want to open your house to a perfect stranger?" I spoke a little more loudly and belligerently than was completely necessary.

She smiled, going from anger to amusement. "I like you. You remind me of me, sort of. You have the same bad qualities."

"Thanks."

"Remember when you got mean?"

"I'm sorry I scared you."

"You didn't scare me. I had to move away to keep from hitting you. Any asshole that turns mean on me can find his own goddam cat."

"You were great."

"I was rather good, wasn't I? Usually I'm not. When people piss me off, I generally hit them or run away. Or both. But there was something about the way you got nasty because you were scared that made me think—I don't know, I felt like I could see into your soul or something. It's because I'm like that, too, I think. Or is that too dumb to make any sense?"

"I don't know." That was the truth. I wasn't sure if it was or wasn't, but I was damn sure it was spooky and weird. I also knew exactly what she meant.

Sardis looked embarrassed. "Anyway, that's why I asked you to stay with me."

"Okay."

"Okay what?"

"Okay, thanks." Mr. Gracious.

"You mean yes?"

She looked sort of happy, so I smiled. "You're nice," I said. "I hope you won't be sorry."

I sure did. I hoped she wouldn't get to know me a little better and decide I was a jerk and get sorry she ever met me. At that moment I hoped that a lot.

On the way back to her place, we stopped for a litter box for Spot and some clothes for me—some regular jeans, some white jeans, and some shirts. Then I made a phone call I didn't want to make—to the fire department. And I learned what I was afraid of learning—somebody'd set my house on fire. Probably with a Molotov cocktail.

On the way back to the place, we stopped for a first
time. He had me locate ... using her bare-conditioning lo-
tion, some white stuff, and some more stuff. Then I made a
phone call (I didn't want to make—to list the apartment)
and I learned what I was trying to learn ... enough to
set my mind on fire. Probably, with a stained carpet ...

CHAPTER 10 The conclusion was inescapable: Whoever killed Jack Birnbaum pretty much had his heart set on killing me next. You'd be surprised how that sort of thing can cause a real sag of the spirits.

The worst thing about it was that I was going to have to find yet another place to live—I couldn't endanger Sardis' life by being in it. It wouldn't be gentlemanly.

"I've gotta leave," I said. "I can't have you harboring a marked man."

"Nonsense," she said. "And too late. Both of us already knew somebody wanted to kill you when I offered to put you up, and neither of us backed out then."

She was right. I wanted to stay with her and I'd been too chickenshit to bring up the danger before, and now I was trying to cover up by being macho. Face it, McDonald, I said to myself, you're full of it.

To Sardis I said, "You're a princess."

"True," she said. "Very true." And she got a kind of smug look like Spot gets when things are going his way.

"I don't want you dead," I said.

"Thank you, sir."

"So let's get this jerk before he gets us."

"My thought exactly." She put some water on for tea and sat down at her kitchen table. I joined her.

"I've been thinking about our conversation last night—about Jack and his 'background checking.' And whether or not he did it routinely. Jack had a list of people to talk to about Lindsay. You and Brissette were on it. So were Joan Hearne, Susanna Flores, and Peter Tillman. Do you know any of them?"

She nodded. "Susanna and Joan, yes. Tillman, a little, but not through Lindsay. I met him at a party once."

"Lindsay was seeing him and he was married."

"So?"

"So he was vulnerable to blackmail. So was Brissette. He had a coke habit, and you had Mr. A&L. Is there anything in either Susanna's or Joan's life that could be used against either of them?"

"Joan's, definitely. She's a former mental patient—took too much acid about fifteen years ago and wound up in the bin. In and out of the bin, matter of fact. Lousy press for a bank veep."

"What about Susanna?"

"I don't know her very well, but she's absolutely straight as far as I know. She and Lindsay and I have been known to have a few drinks and talk a certain amount of girl talk, but she's never let anything slip that could make her vulnerable."

"Do you like her?"

"A lot. Listen, why don't we just ask her? If Jack tried to blackmail her, she'll probably be pretty pissed off and glad to talk about it. Also, she has a vested interest in this thing—two, in fact. She's worried about Lindsay on a personal level and she needs her back for the show."

"Okay, let's ask her."

Sardis made us both some tea and then she reached for the phone. "Susanna? It's Sardis Kincannon." There was a pause.

"No. I haven't heard from her, either. But I've found somebody else who's interested in finding her. I'm afraid it's your competition—a guy named Paul McDonald; he works for the *Chronicle*." Pause. "Yeah, he did quit, but he's back for the time being. Anyway, he worked for Jack Birnbaum and he thinks the way Birnbaum got his information was by blackmailing people." Long pause. "We thought it might be something like that. Thanks, Susanna. I'll be in touch."

"Well?"

"She knows you."

"I don't think so. I'm sure I'd remember."

"I mean your work. She says you're okay."

"That's gratifying." It was, but I was getting impatient. "Did Birnbaum try something with her?"

"Sure did. Her husband's a lawyer who represents some company that was involved in some scandal that *Bay Currents* didn't do a story about. You follow? Anyway, Susanna says she turned down the story without knowing it was a firm her husband represented—one of those deals with a lot of d.b.a's and a.k.a.'s. So it wasn't really a conflict at all, and even if it was, it's pretty weak stuff. But I guess it's all Jack could get. Anyway, he tried that on her and she gave him a piece of her mind and threw him out."

"That settles it then. If he tried to blackmail her, he probably did it with everyone. And that gives just about everyone a motive to kill him."

"But what about Brissette?"

"Good question. Let's try this: Brissette knew something about Lindsay which, under carefully applied pressure, he told Birnbaum. Whatever it was made Birnbaum dangerous to someone. That someone found out he knew and how he found out and killed both him and Brissette."

"And the someone read in the *Examiner* that you were Jack's assistant and figured you knew too. So he tried to kill you."

"We've got to find Lindsay."

"She would seem to be the key."

"Brissette told Jack that Lindsay called him the Wednesday before she disappeared. On a legal matter. But he wouldn't tell Jack what it was."

"You mean that's what Jack said."

"Yes, and what I wrote in the report. So if he did know, he didn't want the client to know. I don't get it."

"Look, let's forget it for a minute. The fact is, Lindsay called him on a legal matter. Unless I'm a little far behind in the Lindsay saga, they weren't close anymore."

"Right. Brissette said he hadn't heard from her in months."

"Okay, she calls him on Wednesday and disappears the following Saturday. Whatever they talked about is something Brissette doesn't want to talk about to anyone else, even a guy who's trying to find her. Maybe she disappeared because she was spooked about something."

"Sounds right."

"So if she was scared, that means she was in danger—or maybe still is."

"But why take Terry? It makes no sense if she's somebody's target."

"I don't know. Could Terry be in danger, too?"

"Possibly. If the threat came from Jacob, then she'd want to take Terry away. But then why would Jacob hire a detective who might find out what he was up to?"

"I've got it! It had something to do with a story she was working on."

I shook my head. "I don't think so. Susanna would have mentioned it."

"Oh." She looked downcast, and then she brightened. "Not necessarily. She might have made up the whole story about Lindsay writing the letter and everything if Lindsay was really undercover or something. So of course she wouldn't have told Birnbaum the truth. And she'd have no reason to know his death was connected with Lindsay, so she wouldn't have told the cops."

I considered.

"Let's go talk to her, Paul. Maybe we can get her to help us."

I couldn't see it, what with her being my professional rival and all, but I had to admit there wasn't a whole hell of a lot else to do—I had to retrace Jack's steps and that was all there was to it. If Sardis could get me an entrée with Susanna, was I going to turn her down?

I wasn't. When she said who we were, the station security guard phoned Susanna and sent us right up. Susanna had a wonderful view of the bay and the Bay Bridge, but that wasn't the exciting part. The Embarcadero Freeway was right outside her window, maybe forty feet away and exactly at eye level.

It's a good thing it was there, too, because everything inside the building was unbelievably depressing. It was a converted warehouse, spiffed up with sweeping stairways, giant photos, and primary colors. It could have been nice. The problem was, the work spaces had no furniture in them—only plastic modular things that seemed to double as desks and partitions. Everyone had his own three-sided module exactly the right size for a moderately slender person, and there were about a million of these half-closets. The place was a high-tech anthill. But that freeway out there was something else again. I couldn't take my eyes off it.

Eventually I had to, though, because staring is rude and

ignoring your hostess ruder still. I turned the old baby blues on Susanna. She was fairly short and maybe twenty pounds overweight, but she carried the weight just right, like pregnant women sometimes do. Her complexion was quite fair and her lips were fullish. Her face was round and very soft. Her breasts were round and looked very soft. Her hair was dark, wavy, and very soft. She was wearing some sort of dress with a flouncy skirt, very soft.

Media, my former field, is full of terrifically interesting people, but not people you'd especially call nice. Susanna Flores looked like she might be about the nicest person in northern California. She looked simple and straightforward—not full of kinks and contradictions like Sardis and me. But that's just how she looked. No telling what she was actually like.

She offered her hand. "Paul," she said, "I've read you for years. You're my favorite writer who ever worked for the *Chronicle*."

That settled it. The woman was an undiscovered saint.

Quickly we brought her up to date, and before we were done, I could tell she was a dead end because she didn't interrupt to tell us why she'd lied to Birnbaum. She hadn't, of course. Lindsay wasn't undercover after all.

"As a matter of fact," said Susanna. "She'd just finished a story. Right before she disappeared."

"Was it an investigative story? Anything that could be dangerous to someone?"

She shook her head. "No. In fact, we ran it after she left. It was just a story about alternative methods of treating cancer."

"Susanna," said Sardis, "had she been depressed or anything lately? I didn't see her for several weeks before she left."

"She seemed it, yes. She was very upset about her breakup with Mike Brissette—oh, God, and now he's dead. It *was* an accident, wasn't it?"

I answered. "It looks like it, but—"

"But maybe not?" She might look simple and straight-forward, but she was a journalist. I hesitated.

As if reading my mind, she said, "Look, Paul, if you think I'm interested in this thing as a story, forget it. In the first place, I haven't got a show without Lindsay. In the second place, I could care less about the goddam story or the goddam show or the whole goddam station. Lindsay's one of my closest friends." Her eyes filled as she spoke.

Sardis and I looked at each other and it was obvious we were of the same mind. I told Susanna all about the attempts on my life and the awful fate of my house and what we thought about Brissette. It didn't exactly ease her mind on the Lindsay question. Her fear popped out of her: "She can't be in danger! She couldn't be!" It was practically a wail.

I was horribly afraid she was—or worse—but I didn't say so. I said, "You were telling us about her breakup with Brissette."

Susanna composed herself. "That was about eight months ago and she never quite seemed to snap out of it— her depression, I mean."

"Didn't she have a new boy friend?"

"Pete Tillman. She started seeing him about a month ago—I mean, a month before she left. But you know—she just didn't seem that interested in him. The only thing that seemed to perk her up was that cancer story she was working on—sometimes she got very exuberant when she was on a good yarn."

"It wasn't that good a story, was it? I mean, it's been done before."

"Lindsay isn't the kind of reporter who only likes a story if it's a potential prizewinner. If she was interested in something, she gave it everything. I mean, she does. God, I sound like she's dead."

Sardis gasped at the sound of the word and I forged

99

ahead quickly. "Think back, Susanna. Was she depressed before she broke up with Brissette?"

"She was, yes. I had the impression they weren't getting along."

"I don't know how to phrase this, exactly, but—did she seem stable?"

"I don't know. I honestly don't know. For months she'd been depressed and withdrawing from me and, I gather, from Sardis and her other friends. Then one day she took Terry and disappeared. It doesn't sound stable, does it? I wish I'd realized sooner."

I could tell this was a train of thought that wasn't exactly new for Susanna and that she felt like hell about it. I kept talking, not wanting to give her time to dwell on it. "How about the week she disappeared—did she seem any different then?"

Susanna brushed her hair behind her ear and paused, her hand over her mouth. "Yes," she said at last. "I think she did. She was sort of high on that cancer story, but that wasn't all. She was very hyper. I mean, she seemed to be working at top speed to finish it. As if she knew she wasn't going to be able to finish it the next week. She was driving so hard one of the cameramen complained."

"And that wasn't like her?"

"No. It was the sort of story that takes two weeks and she did it in one week. It's that simple. Also, she was very edgy that week. As if she had something on her mind. Friday afternoon she was a bear—she was determined to finish the story and she had to meet someone by seven."

"Who?"

"You mean who was she meeting? I don't know. I assumed it was Pete."

"Did she say where she was meeting this person?"

"Why, yes. The Hunan Restaurant. It's around the corner, which meant she could work up until the last minute. It has a bar and lots of people from the station go there after work."

"Did anyone see her there that night?"

"I don't know. I could ask around."

"I think it might be important to know whom she was meeting. Can you see if anyone remembers?"

"Of course. I'll do anything I can to help." She looked very sad, like somebody who's lost a good friend. I hoped like hell she hadn't.

We thanked her and left, Sardis and I, feeling a bit under the weather. Susanna's grief was catching.

"I think," I said, "that I'd better have a talk with Joan. And I think I'd better start flying solo."

If I'd thought that last was going to hurt Sardis' feelings, I was mistaken. "Okay," she said. "I'm feeling slightly guilty about calling in sick. I was thinking I might go to the office and play catch-up." She fished in her purse and came up with a key to her apartment. "Here's an extra in case you get home first. I think I might be pretty late."

It's weird, but I was the one whose feelings were hurt. I'd sort of forgotten Sardis was a busy person with her own life and probably two or three boyfriends. I took the key and thanked her just as the elevator hit bottom.

We walked out in silence and continued walking that way until Sardis screamed. It wasn't a scream, really; just one of those funny syllables like *aaaagh* that people blurt out when they're too surprised to think of a real word.

When she finished blurting *aaagh!*, she said, "Look!" And she pointed to a newsstand with a brand-new *Examiner* in it. The *Ex* has a way of bannering the lead story so at first all I saw was some recession nonsense. And then I saw a picture of a man I didn't know beside a headline that said: DEVELOPER COMMITS SUICIDE. The caption said the man was Peter Tillman.

CHAPTER 11

The story said Tillman was found dead of carbon monoxide poisoning in his car, which was in his garage. It said he had left no note. It said his wife knew of no reason why he would want to kill himself. She was "shocked," it said.

Involuntarily, Sardis and I stared at each other. She had a lot of pain in her face, and worry. "I'll call Joan," she said. "She'll be expecting you. Go right now. Quickly."

She gave me a quick but very tight hug and left to find a phone booth.

I found my own phone booth and looked up the Women's Bank of the Golden State. It was in the financial district, just a few blocks away, so I walked. It may not have been the fastest way to get there, but I figured Joan was safe as long as she was at work, and I needed time to think.

At first, all I could think of was Philip MacDonald, yet another successful mystery writer with my surname. I was thinking of a book by Cousin Phil called *The List of Adrian Messenger*, in which everyone on Adrian's list is found to have died under mysterious circumstances.

I was also thinking about the list I had made of the people involved in the Koehler case. If I didn't live out the day, I was wondering, would Blick find it and would its significance penetrate his thick skull? No, of course he wouldn't. He couldn't find it. It had burned up with everything else I owned.

I made a new list in my head. On it were Jack Birnbaum, Paul Brissette, and Peter Tillman. Somebody wanted me on it. Maybe they wanted Joan, Susanna, and Sardis on it. Maybe Lindsay, too. Or maybe Lindsay was already dead. Or maybe she was the murderer.

But I didn't think so. She might be a bit unstable, but I didn't think she was systematically killing off all her friends. I thought there was something in those reports that was dangerous to someone else. Jacob and Marilyn had read them—did that mean they were in danger, too? Or were they suspects? That was too hard to figure, so I went back to the reports themselves—trying for the umpteenth time to imagine what tiny piece of information they contained that was worth killing three people. Four if you counted me. Were the damn things in code or something? But they couldn't be. I'd written them myself.

I shook my head to clear it. It didn't work. I tried to start at the beginning.

Okay. Someone had killed Birnbaum. Someone had tried to kill me. But maybe Brissette had really fallen down the stairs and Tillman had really committed suicide. I never was good at math, but I tried to figure the probabilities. I did it by counting up all my ex-girlfriends who had died violent deaths within a few hours of each other. The number was zero. All two hundred and eighty-odd of them were healthy as horses. I'll bet nine out of ten people could say that, and the tenth would only have one

JULIE SMITH

dead lover. And nine out of ten of those who did have dead lovers could say with certainty that the deaths were from natural causes. So why should Lindsay be any different? No reason at all. Either Brissette or Tillman or both of them had been murdered. That was the only way it added up.

Most people probably don't figure probabilities that way, but it was good enough to throw a renewed scare into me. I was now approaching the Women's Bank of the Golden State and hoping I'd find Joan in one piece.

I went in. I don't know what I expected, it being a women's bank and all, but it was just like any other bank. There was some wood and some marble and some glass and some of the tellers were men and some were women and that went for the customers as well.

Joan was in her office on the second floor. She had a finely molded face like Lindsay's, but larger lips and much darker hair, which was frizzed but still managed to look neat. She had blue eyes and a tawny, almost orangy complexion. Her dress was a couple of shades lighter than her skin and it had blue stuff at the neck, sleeves, and hem that more or less matched her eyes. Intellectually, I knew the effect was a bit contrived, but given a choice of, say, one hundred fifty interesting things to look at and one of them was Joan in that dress, I'd have chosen Joan. Another thing about the dress—it sort of clung, and not only that, it sort of wrapped around, so that you always thought it would slip a bit and you'd get a glimpse of cleavage or leg, but it never did and you never did.

I figured if I were some guy she was doing business with, I'd be so distracted I'd be helpless. But what the hell—men dress to intimidate; women have to have strategies, too. Whatever works, you know?

"Sardis called about you," said Joan. The hand she gave me was sweaty. "She said you work for the *Chronicle* but I should trust you anyway."

105

I sat down. "Have the police talked to you yet?"

She nodded. "This morning."

"So you know about Birnbaum."

"Yes." Her lips were very tight.

"He tried to blackmail you, didn't he?"

"What are you trying to pull?" The gorgeous shoulders tensed under the clingy dress. Joan's fingers closed around a letter opener, and the way her face looked, I figured she'd just as soon cut my liver out as not.

"Whoa. Joan, whoa. I'm on your side." I spoke softly, as softly as I knew how, but I didn't see the shoulders untensing. The blue eyes were very, very scared.

I tried speaking quickly: "I think Jack tried to blackmail a lot of people. It was his m.o., that's all. I don't want to know what you threatened you with—I mean what information he had, if he had any . . ." I was starting to stammer, but she was relaxing. "I just took a guess, because that was the way he was. I'm not trying to pull anything."

"I'm sorry," she said, and now the eyes were filling with tears. "He was a horrid little sleazoid."

"He did threaten you?"

"Yes." She leaned way back in her chair and looked very sad now. "There is something in my past. Something that could lose my job for me. Or at least keep me from going anywhere from here. It would be the end of my career if anyone knew. Do you understand?"

Since Sardis had filled me in, I understood perfectly. A lady who'd been in and out of loony bins was never going to make it big in banking. If anybody knew, that is. I nodded, to signify understanding.

"Oh, God, I don't know why I'm telling you this." She was getting scared again, probably remembering that I worked for the *Chronicle*.

"Look. Joan. Someone's tried to kill me twice. They burned my house down last night. I'm not here to ruin

106

your career. I'm here to warn you. They may want to kill you, too."

She laughed. I kid you not. She laughed. "Me? Who'd want to kill me?"

"I don't know that anyone would. But let me ask you something. Did Lindsay talk to you about her boy-friends?"

"Some."

"Two of them have died in the last twenty-four hours. Jack Birnbaum had talked to them. He also talked to you."

She laughed again. "You think someone's systematically killing everyone he talked to about Lindsay?"

"No, I don't think it's that. I don't know what to think, except that people who were close to Lindsay are getting killed." I don't know why I used the past tense. I didn't even notice that I did.

Joan stopped laughing and her eyes filled up again. "You think Lindsay's dead?"

"I hope not."

"Why do you think that?" Joan spoke very harshly, almost screaming.

"I didn't say I did."

"She's just gone away, that's all."

"Where?"

She looked completely stricken and then she started sobbing.

"Joan, what's wrong? What did I say?"

She sobbed some more and didn't answer. This was getting to be a habit—about this time yesterday I'd been with Brissette's sobbing assistant, Janet.

"You sound like *him*," Joan said. "He kept asking me where she was."

"Who? Blick?"

She shook her head.

"Birnbaum!"

"He said he'd ruin me if I didn't tell him. I swear to God

I'd have told him if I knew. I just didn't know; that's all there was to it. I don't."

"I believe you. But Lindsay did call the Saturday she left, didn't she? Were you surprised when she told you what she was doing?"

Joan dried her eyes; she was calming down a bit. "No. She'd been talking about it for a long time."

"But why? Why would she do it?"

"She wanted to be with Terry, that's all."

"It seems out of character. Lindsay isn't exactly the maternal type, from what I can gather."

"Have you talked with Jacob?"

"A little, yes."

"Did he tell you anything about Terry?"

"Nothing that impressed me, no. Sardis says she's a smart little kid."

"She's very exceptional. But that isn't what I mean. Jacob didn't happen to mention that she has about six months to live?"

CHAPTER 12

If that didn't explain why Lindsay should get a sudden maternal urge, I didn't know what would.

"No," I said when I'd caught my breath. "He didn't mention it."

"She has leukemia."

"I don't get it. Sardis and Susanna are her best friends and they don't seem to know a thing about it."

"She couldn't talk about it with them. She might have told Sardis, but—well, Sardis had her own problems. She was barely hanging on herself and Lindsay didn't want to make things worse for her. She may not have told her anyway. Lindsay's a very private person. She doesn't like people feeling sorry for her. She likes to think she can work things out herself."

"Is that why she didn't tell Susanna?"

"Partly. But remember, Susanna is her boss. She didn't want Susanna worrying about her and worrying what

109

would happen to the show when Terry went into the hospital and things like that. Also, she always knew there was a possibility she would kidnap Terry and leave Susanna pretty well in the lurch. She'd been desperately trying to get Jacob to give her some time with Terry and she always planned to take it if that was the only way she could get it—if Jacob wouldn't agree, I mean. She didn't want to involve Susanna."

"Did she ever mention trying any 'alternative' treatments for Terry?"

"You mean like Laetrile or something? God, no. Jacob would shit a brick."

I could just bet Jacob would. If there was one thing an establishment scientist would hate, it would be cancer quacks—especially within several thousand miles of his sick daughter.

Here was what I imagined had happened: Lindsay had suggested the cancer quack show because, in her desperation, she hoped to find out about something that might help Terry. She did in fact see something she thought was worth trying. She put it to Jacob; he shat a brick; and she figured her last chance to save the daughter she hardly knew was to kidnap her and take her to the quack. All I had to do was figure out which quack it was.

I asked Joan one more question: "Did you tell the police about Terry's illness?"

"No. They didn't ask why Lindsay left, just where she went."

My lack of confidence in Blick remained unshaken.

I said good-bye to Joan and walked back to Susanna's station. I figured she might know which of the quacks Lindsay had liked. At least she could run the show for me and I could look over the candidates. As I walked, I turned things over in my head.

Little Terry's illness explained an awful lot. Why Lindsay'd been depressed lately, for openers, and why she'd been withdrawing from her friends. Why she did a bizarre thing like kidnap her own daughter and leave her job. And if my hunch was right, why she did it when she did it.

But it didn't come close to explaining why three people had been killed. It also didn't explain why the Koehlers had reneged on our interview. If Jacob was worried that his precious daughter was in the hands of some quack, why wouldn't he do anything he could to get her back? Could he have thought publicity would put her in further danger? Who knew? He was an odd duck.

And so, for that matter, was Joan. After her alternate laughings and cryings, I was damned glad to be heading toward the soothing presence of Susanna.

I found her staring out at her freeway. Sardis had called her about Tillman. Also, Blick had been there. She was too upset to work and I was going to have to upset her further. "Susanna," I said, "I've found out why Lindsay took Terry and left. But it's pretty awful."

"Tell me."

"Terry's sick. She's going to die."

It took her about half a second to put that together with what she already knew. "Cancer!"

I nodded.

"That explains why she was so excited about that show." Her face was glowing. She was positively cheered up. "*And* why she left. And where she probably is."

I breathed a man-size sigh of relief. I'd thought I was in for more tears. But Susanna was a journalist, and it was probably no accident she'd become one—she was just like all the others I knew. The thing she hated worst was not knowing something. She could take bad news a lot better than suspense and unanswered questions.

"You think," I said, "that she's taken Terry to some cancer quack?"

"Sure. The question is which one."

"I thought you might have some ideas on that. Were there any that particularly impressed her?"

Susanna shook her head. "Not that I know of. Let's ask the cameraman." She called him in and we did. He said that while she hadn't been her usual cynical self on the story, had seemed much more open-minded than usual, she hadn't exactly singled out any of the quacks for praise.

We decided to watch the tape of the show. Seeing Lindsay on screen was as much a pleasure as it always had been. Her hair was taffy-colored, her eyes green, her voice low and lovely. But the best part, as always, was the sense of quick intelligence at work, with a stark honesty behind it. Like Walter Cronkite, she had the knack of making you believe her.

But the show gave us no hints whatsoever—if Lindsay liked one of her quacks well enough to take her daughter to him, the home TV audience didn't get inkling one. She was professional as hell.

Watching the show wasn't a total waste of time, though. We got the names of the guys she'd talked to—eight of them, scattered from Mexico to Reno. If she put that show together in a week, no wonder the tech crew complained.

Anyway, I now had the names of the eight most likely quacks (though maybe Lindsay had gone to one she didn't interview), but where did that get me? I could hardly phone them and ask to speak to her—for one thing, who knew what name she was using? For another, she certainly wouldn't be taking calls. The only thing to do was talk Joey Bernstein into letting me go prowl around the various cure-halls—if Lindsay could do it in a week, so could I.

But Susanna thought that was a dumb idea. "People are dying at the rate of one a day," she pointed out. "We don't have a week."

"What else can we do?"

"We have to tell the cops."

I started to answer, but I couldn't think of a thing to say. Seizing the advantage, she kept talking: "Your life is in danger, Paul. And so is Sardis' as long as you're staying with her."

There was a chance, of course, that her own and Joan's were too. And maybe Jacob's and Marilyn's. She was unquestionably right. If Lindsay was at some hospital, the cops would find her in about twenty-four hours. And if I'd given Blick the damn Koehler file in the first place, Brissette and Tillman might still be alive. This was no time for wasting time.

I picked up the phone and got Blick. "Howard," I said. "I have information that may lead to the arrest and conviction of a killer."

"Stick it where the sun don't shine, McDonald."

"I'm not kidding, Howard. This is big."

"Yeah? So's your dick."

Now *what* was that supposed to mean? I ignored it. "Stay there. I'm coming down to the Hall."

The Hall of Justice was what I meant. What a building. Not only was the cop shop there, so was the DA's office, all the Municipal Courts, several Superior Courts, city prison, and county jail. It was worth your life just to ride in the elevators.

But I did, clear up to Homicide, where I did not expect to be received cordially and where I was not disappointed.

Blick's potato face was unsmiling. I started out slow: "I heard the Koehlers' case reports were stolen too."

"Now how'd you hear that?"

"But I presume the Koehlers filled you in on what they said."

"How come you're so concerned all of a sudden? You coulda filled me in your own sweet self."

"Did they tell you that both Mike Brissette and Peter Tillman were ex-lovers of Lindsay Hearne?"

"What's it to you, McDonald?"

113

God, he was making it hard. "Did you talk to either of them before they died?"

"What do you think, you son of a bitch? If I didn't, whose fault was it?"

"Look, Howard—I should have given you the damn file, okay? I'm sorry, okay? What do I have to do, send you a dozen roses? Look, I'm here because I think I know how to find Lindsay Hearne. That's one reason. Another reason is, I think three murders might have been committed instead of one. I think I might have mentioned to you that somebody tried to kill me once. Last night he burned my house down, which I took to mean he was trying again. But that's not a reason why I'm here, because you told me you didn't give a shit about it. However, if somebody's killed three people and tried to kill me, maybe he'll kill somebody else and I thought you might give a shit about that. So that's another reason I'm here."

"You lost your house, huh?"

I nodded, thinking he might say something sympathetic, like "tough break." He didn't. He yawned. "So how do I find the Hearne broad?"

"Don't you care what was in the case reports? Can't you see I'm trying to tell you, asshole?"

"Well, now, that surprises me, McDonald. I thought you had some sort of confidentiality agreement with your client. I thought I was supposed to get that information from Koehler."

He was really rubbing my nose in it. Well, hell. At least I'd called him asshole and he'd only called me son of a bitch. But he was still a few insults ahead of me. I decided to take this opportunity to even the score.

"Howard," I said, "you are an unmitigated scumbag; an unparalleled douchebag; a double-dog, triple-crown asshole of heroic proportions. You have the brains of a nematode; your face looks like a potato; and if you are married, your wife must be a . . ."

He was getting redder and redder. Now he doubled up his fist.

". . . saint," I finished.

"Huh?" he said. He was so surprised he lost his rhythm completely. He caught on right away that he couldn't hit me for calling his wife a saint, but by the time he realized he had ample provocation on his own account, he was worn out from all that thinking and didn't have the strength. He just sat there and looked confused.

"I think I'll be going," I said, and got out of my chair.

"Sit your butt down, McDonald."

I complied.

"Now, to the best of your recollection, what was in those reports?"

"I thought you didn't need to know, Howard. I thought Koehler told you." It just popped out. Too late I realized we were getting right back on the same merry-go-round. So I took corrective steps. "Look, let's be reasonable. I'll trade you what I know for what you know."

"McDonald, are you crazy? I already know what was in the goddam reports."

"You need confirmation and you know it."

"Yeah, and you're going to give it to me. There never was any question of that and you know it."

"Tell me something, Howard—was there digitalis mixed in with Jack's saccharine, like I said?"

"What's that got to do with the price of persimmons?"

"Well, I was kind of wondering, you know, if a digitalis tablet really looks like a saccharine pill—I mean, wouldn't they make them a different size so you wouldn't mistake one for another?"

"Now how many people put them in the same bottle, jerkoff?"

"So Jack's were in the same bottle."

"You ain't as smart as you think you are, McDonald. But you ain't wrong all the time."

"Fine. Now about those reports—"

"You mean that's what you wanted to know?"

"Part of it. As I recall, Koehler gave Birnbaum four names to check out—Joan Hearne, Susanna Flores, and Mr. and Mrs. Timothy A. Hearne."

"Only four?"

"Oh, yeah. I forgot. Five. Sardis Kincannon was on the list, but Jack never got around to her. She was on vacation at the time in, uh—"

"Maui. Well, Maui and Honolulu. She stayed with some friends on Oahu for a few days."

Good. Very good. I had had kind of a block about checking Sardis' alibi—for some reason, it was just something I didn't want to do. It wouldn't exactly have been betraying a trust or anything, but I didn't want to do it.

So now I knew two things—so far, Jacob had told Blick the truth and Blick had done my dirty work. He was showing off, letting me know he'd checked Sardis' alibi, and now I knew it was good. Not that I'd ever doubted.

I went on and told Blick how Joan had said Lindsay called her the day of the snatch, and also how she'd supplied Peter Tillman's name, and how Tillman had said Lindsay broke a date with him the night before the snatch, and how Susanna had told about Lindsay calling in sick and had mentioned Mike Brissette, and how Brissette had said he'd recently talked to Lindsay on a "legal matter" but wouldn't say what it was, and how the Timothy A. Hearnes had been thoroughly checked by Atlanta operatives.

Every now and then I left out some little thing, the way I left out Sardis' name, to see if it would make Blick ask a question. It did, every time. That meant Jacob had filled him in thoroughly, telling exactly the same story I was telling. Unless, of course, he'd embellished.

When I was done, Blick said, "Is that *all*?"

I couldn't tell whether he was jacking me around or whether Koehler had told him stuff that I didn't know about. Stuff that was either true or that he'd made up.

"That's everything I wrote," I said. "If there's anything—"

Blick waved a meaty hand. "Forget it. So where's Lindsay Hearne?"

"Howard, about those pills. Do you think you could call the crime lab and—"

"Not a chance in hell."

"It's been nice talking to you. See you around sometime."

"The pills were shaved, douchebag."

"What?"

"Somebody took a knife and very carefully carved them into smaller pills that looked like saccharine tablets. That's what you wanted to know, isn't it?"

I just nodded, I was so shocked. It was true I'd already said I wanted to know about the pills, but I was amazed that Blick remembered and that he'd remembered to ask the crime lab in the first place. Maybe he'd been taking smart lessons.

"So where is she?" he asked. "The Hearne babe."

I told him about Lindsay and the cancer quacks, extracted a promise to let me know when he found her, and turned over the eight names.

Then I left, thinking I still owed him two or three after that interview. Twice I'd come damn close to leaving without telling him what I'd come there to tell him; he'd goaded me with a lot more relish than good sense. What the hell kind of cop would do a thing like that? What kind of man was so stubborn, so hell-bent on revenge, that he'd endanger other people's lives to get it? Hell of an interesting topic.

I may never start liking Blick, but that day I started

giving him credit—he's taught me a thing or two abut myself by setting an even worse example than I could.

It was getting close to six o'clock, so I thought I'd go see if Sardis felt like dinner pretty soon. She'd said she was going to be working late, and I figured she'd still be at work.

At that time of night you have to ring a bell to get in—I mean aboard. I did, said who I wanted, and someone directed me to Sardis' cubicle. She was drawing something.

"Hi," I said.

"Paul!" She looked alarmed. "What are you doing here?"

"I just thought we could . . . I mean—"

"Listen, you shouldn't have come here. We *really* shouldn't be seen together."

She was right, of course. But I hadn't realized she was so nervous about it, and finding out made me feel bad. I guess I must have hung my head or something.

Sardis mustered up an unconvincing smile. "Sorry," she said. "We can talk about it later. Okay?"

"Sure," I said. "See you at home."

The thing was getting to her. Maybe because of Tillman's death. Whatever the reason, she was much more nervous than she had been. I was going to have to think about finding another place to stay. It was the only gentlemanly thing to do.

No, it wasn't. I remembered she didn't have her car. I went back to her tiny office. "Sardis?"

She looked at her watch. "You're still here."

"I thought if you want to call me when you're through, I could come get you."

She smiled, again a little thinly, I thought. "No, thanks. I went home and got my car after we left Susanna's. Now you run along."

I did, not feeling so hot.

I headed toward the parking lot two piers down from the Pandorf boat, thinking I didn't like the idea of Sardis walking along the Embarcadero alone. It was foggy and spooky even now, getting more so by the second. And it was practically deserted. There was only one other guy there now. You could easily step back in the shadows and hide until your victim came along if you had that sort of thing in mind. I did it, just to get the feel of it.

The other guy—my projected victim—passed me. It was Steve Koehler.

CHAPTER 13

Stunned, I watched him go to Pandorf Associates. I don't know why I was so stunned, really. He was having his C.I. done and had a perfect right to be there. On the other hand, maybe he'd come to kill Sardis. There were other people on the boat, so he wouldn't do it there. I decided to wait where I was.

In about ten minutes they came out arm in arm. Sardis and Steve. I let them walk past me and then I followed them to the parking lot. They got in Steve's car while I got in mine. They pulled out and turned right on the Embarcadero. So did I. That was the way to Sardis' house, which was the only place I had to go. So, of course, I turned right.

After a while Steve turned left. He was no longer heading toward Sardis', but I turned left, too. I admitted to myself that I was following him. I was at loose ends and not getting anywhere with the story and didn't know what

121

to do next, and I was a little bit afraid for Sardis. That was why I was doing it, I said to myself. It was probably partly true, too. The fact that I am also a jealous and small-minded person who wanted to find out exactly what Sardis was doing with that jerk probably had no more than about ninety percent to do with it.

Steve had some sort of small, light-colored car. I got a most perfunctory look at the car that tried to hit me, but I could swear it was something like Steve's. I myself was at the wheel of a beige Toyota even as I thought this, and Sardis had a cream-colored Honda. I wondered idly if I should also look at Jacob's, Marilyn's, Joan's, and Susanna's cars. Maybe I could rule out anybody who had a big, dark car. But I decided against it. You could always borrow, steal, or rent a car if you wanted to kill somebody. You probably would, in fact. Maybe you'd even hire somebody to drive it.

Okay, so I didn't really have anything on Steve Koehler. But he seemed as good a suspect as anybody, and I didn't like the idea of Sardis being with him. She was my hostess, after all, and my life was in her hands. Maybe she was conning me. Maybe she had lured Lindsay to Hawaii and bumped her off there and now she and Steve were in cahoots to . . . to what? I was being dumb. I was still trying to justify following an innocent citizen out on a harmless date.

I wasn't succeeding, but I was still following. I followed that small, light-colored car right to downtown San Francisco, where it turned into the Downtown Center Garage at Mason and O'Farrell. I put my press parking card on my dashboard, parked illegally, and waited for them.

They came out and walked up Mason to Geary and crossed it. Then they kept walking until they got to the Pacific Plaza Hotel. I stopped following when they went in. It was getting undignified.

And it got a lot worse. I waited for them. Of course, I didn't think of it that way at the time. I realized it had been a long time since I'd been to the One-Act Theater Company, which is right across from the Pacific Plaza. I thought maybe I'd just have a sandwich at the Stage Door Deli and then take in the show.

The One-Acters usually present three or four one-act plays, just as their name suggests they might, loosely related by some common theme. Tonight it was "Three Women Playwrights," which is about as loosely related as you can get.

The first two were pretty good, and Mittie Smith, my favorite local actress, was the star of the third, so it promised to be even better.

But for some reason I left at intermission. I couldn't explain it. I just had this wild urge to go outside and get some air. I stayed reasonably back in the shadows while I was getting the air, and I took in lungful after lungful. I didn't really feel like I'd done quite enough breathing until Steve and Sardis came out of the hotel, maybe fifteen or twenty minutes later.

So Sardis had spent a couple of hours in a hotel with Steve Koehler. Big deal. There was probably a conference room in there where they were having a meeting.

Anyway, she'd been there with him and you'd think that would be enough to satisfy just about anyone's curiosity, but you'd be wrong. I followed them all the way back to the parking lot where Sardis' car was, watched them kiss—quite passionately, I might add—and then watched Sardis get in her own small, light-colored car.

Then, having gone that far, I followed her home. By an incredible stroke of luck, I found a parking place not more than a half a block away from hers. But I thought I'd wait to go in till after she went in. I hadn't yet decided whether or not to confront her with what I knew and I didn't want it to be obvious that I'd tailed her.

I watched her get out, lock her car, walk around it, and step up on the sidewalk. And then I saw a man step out of a doorway and walk toward her. Fast. I had to look away while I was getting out of my car, but I thought I saw him grab her arm and I thought I saw them start to struggle. Then I heard a godawful noise—the police whistle Sardis carried on her key ring.

The man started running—right towards me. By this time I was running too, and I guess he figured I was going for him, so he turned around and ran the other way, around the corner. San Francisco being the kind of city it is, there was about a fifty-fifty chance of the route he chose being uphill. Uphill it was, and while I believe women find me all the more masculine owing to a trifling tendency to burliness, someone who meant to be unkind might suggest that I ought to lose weight. Thus I huffed and I puffed and I watched him put a couple of city blocks between us.

Feeling ridiculous, I gave up and ambled back down the hill, trying to learn to breathe again on the way. Sardis was waiting at the bottom, looking white. She flung herself at me and I caught her, mumbling something like "Sorry I didn't catch him." She mumbled something like "Pish-tush," and we didn't say anything else, just held on to each other, until we got inside.

Sardis' apartment was small but very cozy—a brown velvet sofa, a rocking chair, quilts, that sort of stuff. At that moment it looked more inviting than the sumptuous den of the Count of Monte Cristo. Sardis poured us both a brandy, and I tossed mine back and held out my glass for more. I act macho when I'm terrified.

Sardis sat down in her rocker. "He spoke to me, Paul. He knew me."

"What did he say?"

"He said, 'Where's Lindsay Hearne? I won't hurt you if you tell me.' And he grabbed my arm."

124

"Did you recognize him?"

She shuddered. "No. He had on a stocking mask. Horrible."

"How about the voice?"

"He whispered."

"Are you sure it was a man?"

"Oh, yes. A big one."

I sighed. "Shall we call the cops?"

She shook her head vigorously. "Let's not. There's nothing they can do except make us wait for forty-five minutes till they get here, and then take a report. I can't deal with them now—tomorrow I'll call Inspector Blick and tell him it happened."

I was relieved. The last thing I wanted in that velvety, quilty, cozy place was cops. Also, I didn't want the interruption. Sardis and I had a lot to talk about.

I started out nice and slow-like, kind of subtle: "How long have you been sleeping with Steve Koehler?"

"What?" she said. She looked as if I'd asked her whether Spot barked much. The question didn't seem to compute at all. Suddenly I felt like the two-bit turd I was.

"I meant—uh—well, I went to the show at the One-Act Theater and I happened to see you walking out of a hotel with him. I just thought, well . . . you might like to tell me about it."

"I might, yes. First we had the carpaccio. And then he had the duck and I had some pasta. Fantastic. And then . . ."

"There's a restaurant in that little hotel?"

Again she looked as if she thought I was pulling her leg. "Donatello—haven't you been?"

"On my income, I haven't even heard of it." If I spoke testily, it was because I was so embarrassed at being such a dumb shit that I felt the need to take it out on somebody.

But Sardis didn't seem to notice. "Anyway," she said, "it was strictly a business date. We had some things to clear up about his C.I."

"Do you always kiss your clients so enthusiatically?"

"(A)," she said, "I do not kiss my clients at all, and (B) I do not understand what the hell you're getting at."

"(A)," I said, "I saw you kiss Koehler, and (B) what about Mr. A&L?"

For a moment she didn't speak. She just stood there looking as if I'd told her an earthquake had killed all her living relatives. Her cheeks flamed a becoming fuchsia. It was very scary. When she spoke, she spoke very slowly: "I'm going to ask you to apologize for B and explain A."

I had to admire her for that. She had paused to figure out exactly what she wanted from me and it was exactly the right thing. Reasonable as hell. Any peaceable adult would have obeyed instantly.

I said, "Why the hell should I?"

"Because you're behaving like a prick and I—"

"Who the hell are you to tell me—" The rest of her sentence stopped me:

"I don't really think it's your natural state."

She just wasn't taking any of the bait. There I was, ready to alienate her forever, get her to throw me out, convince her I was a madman and, when you got right down to it, a prick. I could have brooded about it for the next six months. And here Sardis wanted to be reasonable.

Of course, none of that actually went through my mind at the time. I was too worked up, not thinking at all, just feeling. I started out feeling angry, of course, and that feeling progressed right on to angrier. But Sardis had got to me and now I just felt silly and ashamed.

"I'm sorry," I said, "about Mr. A&L. I don't know why I said it."

"It's okay."

Neither of us spoke for a minute and then Sardis did again: "If you ever speak to me like that again, I'll detooth you."

"I'm sorry," I said again.

"What did you mean about seeing me kiss Steve Koehler?"

"Nothing. I don't know why I said that, either."

"Dammit, you didn't just decide to go to the theater and just happen to see us come out of that hotel. You tailed us."

Now that I really was ashamed of. I didn't want to admit it worth a damn. Yet it was I who had brought up the good-night kiss. I certainly seemed to want it both ways.

"Look," she said, "I could get my feelings hurt, but I'm trying not to. I'm reminding myself that there have been two attempts on your life and that you never saw me before yesterday and you don't know if I'm concealing Lindsay's whereabouts or if I helped her snatch the kid or killed her or what. You've got every right to be suspicious. So I've got an idea. Why don't I just tell you the names of the various places I stayed in Hawaii and you can check my alibi for yourself."

"That wasn't why I followed you." I was so taken aback I had made the tactical error of blurting out the truth. I tried to recover: "You seemed pretty eager to get rid of me when I came over to the boat."

"I know it seemed that way. But I wanted you out of there before Koehler got there. I figure the fewer people who know you and I know each other the better. But look. You don't have to believe me. You'll feel better if I give you those names."

She was being so decent I couldn't stand it. I said, "Blick told me he checked you out. I know your alibi's good."

"I don't understand."

I shrugged.

"Well, why the hell did you follow me then?"

"Out of plain, childish jealousy."

She looked amazed. And very confused, as if she were trying to decide whether I was a madman or just somebody with a couple of kinks. Apparently, she decided on the latter, as she came down unexpectedly with a fit of the giggles.

"What's so funny?"

She kept on giggling. "You looked so desperate when you said that, like you thought you'd be struck dead. Didn't you ever tell the truth before?"

"Not if it made me look this bad."

She was still giggling. "It's not so bad. I think it's sort of flattering."

I seized the advantage: "I wouldn't follow just anybody, you know."

She crossed the room and stood close to me. "See that you don't. And one other thing."

I moved closer to her and put a hand on her shoulder. I put my mouth very close to hers. "What?" I whispered.

"Follow me again and I'll cut your spleen out."

"Kiss Koehler again and I'll cut yours out."

"I was an innocent bystander. He planted one on me."

Our arms went around each other. "It didn't look that way to me."

"Well, it was."

"I distinctly saw you—" I didn't get to finish because she planted one on me. I saw how these things could happen.

That night I didn't sleep on the sofa. In fact, I hardly slept at all.

Sardis and I were very good together. I couldn't remember being as excited by a woman as I was by her. I couldn't remember wanting somebody so much for so long (forty-eight hours, wasn't it?) and having it turn out so well. Come to think of it, the way my life had been going, I couldn't remember much about women at all.

But I'm being silly. The truth is, it was a night of flashing lights and calliope music. The next morning I felt as if I'd risen from the dead.

I felt so good I cooked breakfast—cheese omelets, home

fries; I even whipped up some biscuits. It was Saturday, so we had champagne with our orange juice. Neither of us even brought up the subject of Lindsay until the paper was read.

But the last Sardis knew was that Tillman was dead and I'd gone off to warn Joan. She had to be brought up to date. So when she had a sufficient amount of champagne inside her, I told her about Terry's illness and about sending Blick to find Lindsay in Quackland.

Once over the shock, she remembered something that seemed related. Steve Koehler had consistently refused to reveal the nature of Kogene's projected product, even to her. But last night, for the first time, he had hinted broadly about it.

"I told him flat out I couldn't design a logo without knowing what he's selling and he gave me all this garbage about how it should signify health and feeling good and the fountain of youth. And then he said I should imagine feeling the worst kind of hopelessness, being absolutely sure you were going to die, and then getting a second chance. That was what the logo should convey, he said. So I said, 'Like if you had cancer and somebody came up with a cure for it?' And he looked me right in the eye and said, 'Exactly like that.'"

"It's got to be a cancer cure."

She nodded. "He all but spelled its name."

"But it's something other than interferon."

"Right. But I'm afraid we digress. I just wanted to tell you while we were on the subject. Back to Lindsay—did Jacob and Marilyn mention Terry's illness when you went out to see them?"

"No. And I think that's pretty strange, don't you?"

"Paul, there's something creepy about all this."

"More than one thing."

"I mean about Jacob."

"You said he's always been crazy."

She sighed. "True. I keep forgetting he can't be expected to behave like a normal person."

All of a sudden my brain felt tired. "Oh, hell," I said. "Let's go back to bed."

And that's how the weekend went. I don't mean to give you the impression it was nothing but speculation about the case interspersed with galvanic, white-hot lovemaking. It was nothing of the sort. That was the last speculating we did until Monday.

After two days of unspeakable bliss, you can imagine how eager I was to reenter the world of journalism. But Sardis went to her office, so it was either that or play with my toes.

I had no idea in hell what to do next. But I figured I'd better let Joey Bernstein know I was still alive, just because it was good psychology, so I ambled into my office. And there I found a message from none other than Jacob Koehler, the Nobel laureate himself.

CHAPTER 14

The message was dated that day, Monday. Jacob had called me first thing that morning. I was flattered.

I dialed Kogene Systems, asked for Jacob Koehler, and waited confidently. The receptionist said she would check to see if he was in. Then she said he wasn't.

The number he'd given me was the office, but undaunted, I called his house. No answer.

I was getting annoyed.

There being nothing else to do, I brought Joey up to date, telling him about the fire and little Terry's leukemia and how I had single-handedly figured out where Lindsay was and put the cops on the trail.

No matter how much you give them, editors always want more. Joey asked if I'd checked with Blick to see if he'd found her. The truth was, I hadn't thought of it because he said he'd call me, which just shows you how overconfident a person can get when a woman like Sardis looks at him twice. Obligingly, I called Blick.

He was his usual charming self: "I don't want to talk to you, you son of a bitch."

"What'd I do now?"

"Look. We had a little personal difference or two, so you gave me a bum steer to get even. Very funny, McDonald. Very amusing. Only I used a lot of man-hours checking out those addresses you gave me, and that was taxpayers' money. Maybe you think I'm a dumb cop, hotshot, but I take my job seriously. I can't prove two people wouldn't of got killed if you hadn't played games with me, but I can prove I wasted a weekend checking out some phony lead for some two-bit intellectual. Next time I see your fat face I hope it's smashed in about eight or ten places."

Two-bit intellectual! I wished he'd go back to "asshole". I should've hung up then. There was no reasoning with that ape. But like a fool, I tried anyway: "It was an honest mistake, Howard."

"Like hell."

"I thought she'd be there, I swear to God."

"You know little Terry's father, Jacob? He says the kid ain't sick."

"The kid's aunt says she is."

"The kid's aunt's a loony."

Joan might be at that. She certainly had been. She still changed moods a lot faster than the average person and sometimes she displayed what the shrinks call "inappropriate affect." But even if she was a loony, what reason would she have to make up a story about Terry's fatal illness? To throw us off the track, so we'd waste time looking for Lindsay in the wrong place? In that case, why not tell the police instead of me? I didn't get it, and that made me cross. But since I was a two-bit intellectual, my finely tuned wit was in no way affected by my mood. I handled Blick as brilliantly as always.

"Takes one to know one," I said. And hung up.

I tried calling Jacob again. He still wasn't in. I asked when he would be. I might as well not have bothered.

The hell with it. I'd go there and wait for him. Unless he was sick—in which case he'd be home, which he wasn't—he was bound to turn up soon. He was probably at the dentist's or something.

So I got in my small, light-colored car, drove to Emeryville, and stormed Kogene.

"Is Jacob in?" I asked, using his first name like we were tennis partners.

"Sorry, he's not," said the receptionist. "I don't know if he's coming in or not."

"Isn't that sort of unusual? I mean, I thought he came in every day."

She shrugged. "Dr. Koehler does pretty well what he pleases."

"I think I'll wait awhile if you don't mind. See if he turns up."

"Of course. Can I get you some coffee?"

I said yes and she disappeared and came back with it. She seemed a nice lady. Probably she was the one who'd brought in the stack of elderly *Reader's Digests* that were all there were to read.

Within, say, half an hour, I knew a new way to lose weight, a half dozen new jokes, and some interesting facts about teenage alcoholics. It was stimulating, but I had a murderer to catch. Maybe Steve or Marilyn would know where Jacob was.

I asked if I could see Steve.

"Mr. Koehler is in a meeting," she said, looking infinitely regretful.

"How about Marilyn?"

"I'll see." Again she got up and walked out.

She came back more regretful still. "Dr. Markham is in the same meeting."

I stuck it out for about another half hour. Then I had the nice lady check to see if the meeting was over, which it wasn't. So I told her I'd give Jacob a ring and I left.

I'm just not good at waiting. There's something about it that makes my muscles tense up and gives me a headache and generally makes me want to chew up a few sets of crockery. So maybe I pulled out of my parking place and drove towards San Pablo Avenue a little more carelessly than I should have and a good deal faster than the law allows. It was tempting because there were no other cars on the street. Emeryville's like that—sometimes completely deserted, sometimes crawling with mile-high semis. Right now it was deserted and I took advantage of it.

Park, the street I was on, dead-ended at San Pablo, where there was a traffic light. The fact that it was green probably saved my life. Because when I braked to turn onto San Pablo, nothing happened. That is, nothing I wanted to happen happened. I neither stopped nor started, for I had no brakes. I jerked the emergency brake. It offered no resistance and no comfort. I started taking that turn a lot faster than seemed sensible if I wanted the car to remain on four wheels, so I rethought it, took lightning action, and found myself headed for one of Emeryville's more venerable poker parlors. I realized I probably wasn't going to hit it, though. I'd probably hit one of the cars parked in front of it, or if I missed those, I'd go up over the curb and the impact of that would probably flip me over. Or maybe it wouldn't; maybe I *would* hit the poker parlor.

The next few seconds really taught me the meaning of sweaty palms; if I thought I'd had them at my high school prom, I was mistaken. The steering wheel was so slippery I could hardly get a grip on it. And getting a grip on it was about the most important thing I was ever going to have to do.

134

I definitely didn't want to take my chances with the poker parlor. It was a hell of a lot bigger than I was. It probably ate small, light-colored cars for breakfast. So there was nothing to do but change course.

If I could just get the car going left, there was a sort of alleyway that led to the Bank of America parking lot next door to the poker parlor. It was nearly as wide as a street and perhaps it was one. Maybe it kept on going past the parking lot. Maybe I could just get on it and kind of coast until my car stopped. That is, unless another car was coming out of it toward San Pablo. From where I was, I couldn't see past the bank's parking lot and I had no idea what further horrors lay on the other side. However, if I got in there and there was something coming at me, maybe I could just rethink things again and head into the parking lot. It was true that there were a lot of cars parked there, and if I missed those, there was the Bank of America itself, but it would probably be no harder on a Toyota than the poker parlor.

Frantically, I tried to turn the wheel, all slippery and contrary. I kept trying and it kept slipping, but I didn't let that bother me. I kept after that son of a bitch.

And eventually man won out over machine. I got the car going vaguely in the right direction, but it was really a hell of an ambition I had. I had to turn the car left, which I'd just managed to do, and then right again, very fast, going about thirty-five or forty. I'm sure there are drivers that could do it. I'll bet if I got the chance, even I could probably do it next time, now that I've had some practice.

But the truth is, that time it just didn't quite work out right. I jumped up on the curb on the poker parlor side of the alleyway and mercifully didn't flip over. I just went up high and then did it again as my back wheels followed the front ones, leaping over a little triangle of sidewalk and landing in the target alleyway. So far, so good.

But then I lost control of the car. I couldn't get the

sucker to go right and straighten out, no matter how hard I tried. I was headed right for the parking lot and a little old lady was just backing a forest-green Rabbit out of her space. The Rabbit was the only thing between me and the Bank of America, and in retrospect, thank God for it. But I wasn't thanking anybody for it at the time. I was wishing like hell I wasn't about to plow right into it.

About then it occurred to me simply to turn off the ignition. I don't know why I thought of it then and not before, but I'd like to think it was good instincts. I think that if I'd turned it off before that, something a lot worse would have happened. But I'd lost a great deal of momentum going over the curb and a sudden stop wouldn't be quite so devastating. Like I said, I didn't think that; I just knew it by instinct.

So I turned it off, but that didn't mean I stopped. No sirree. It just meant I didn't hit the Rabbit very hard. Its rear got a bit smashed and so did my front, but neither car turned into an accordion, which was enough to make me want to get down on my knees and shout "Hallelujah!". But the Rabbit-owner didn't see it that way.

I'd guess she was closer to seventy than sixty-five and no more than five feet four, but she came out swinging. I got out of my car as quickly as I could, shaking like I was, and started over to her, all solicitude, but she met me halfway. A right to the solar plexus. A left to the kidney. A foot to the shin. And language! She made Blick look like a Sunday school teacher.

I flailed around, thinking if I could catch her wrists, I could stop the terrible hammering pain that I was experiencing, but my palms were still too sweaty to get any purchase, or something. Also, I felt sick and I was seeing double, sort of. Anyway, not seeing very well. Those were some of the factors that contributed to what happened next, I guess. Or it may simply be that I'm big but not tough.

Because the next thing I remember is lying on the ground and being stomped on.

Some onlookers must have pulled her off me. Anyway, my next memory is of sitting up, knowing I was about to throw up, realizing that my glasses weren't on my face, feeling bewildered, and trying to answer the ornery-looking dude who was inquiring about my health.

I haven't the least idea what Mrs. Rabbit-Owner looked like, but I can remember my nurse perfectly. He was big, black, and scarred on the right cheek. He was wearing a leather jacket and one of those multicolored, knitted skullcaps tough black guys wear to make them look tougher. The kind of guy I'd expect to mug old ladies, and here he was taking care of me after a mugging administered by an old lady. For about three weeks afterward I hardly thought in stereotypes at all.

As it happened, I didn't throw up, did find my glasses, didn't have anything broken, and regained my powers of speech after ten or fifteen minutes.

The cops came and went; Mrs. Rabbit-Owner apologized for turning me black and blue; I assured her I was insured, and then I waited for a tow truck, caught a ride to a body shop, and stuck around for a while. I had a pretty good idea why the brakes failed, but I wanted confirmation.

CHAPTER 15 I got it—
my brake lines had been cut. That made three attempts on
my life in two days. Some guys get nervous about stuff
like that.

Me, I merely took leave of my senses. Meaning I called
Blick to fill him in. You can imagine how that went.

On the whole, it was rather a discouraging morning.
This was the score: one failure to reach Jacob by phone,
one failure to find Lindsay at a hospital, half a dozen insults
from Blick, one failure to reach Jacob by personal appearance, one sickle-swipe from the grim reaper, one smashed
Toyota, one severe beating from one new enemy, and half
a dozen more insults from Blick.

Some guys let stuff like that get them down. Me, I went
to the office, crawled under the city desk and arranged my
ursine frame in a fetal position.

I had to lie there twenty minutes before Joey relented
and offered to buy me lunch. It was the classic two-martini

one and it did me a world of good. That and Joey's promise to lend me a company car for the time being gave me strength to return my phone calls.

There were two messages—both from Susanna. I figured I knew what she was calling about and I hated to ruin her day, but it's rude not to return calls, so I did. And told her Lindsay was still missing.

"I thought as much, since I hadn't heard from you." She sighed. "But I do have a tiny piece of information for you. Two, in fact. One of the cameramen saw her in the Hunan Restaurant the night before she took off."

"No kidding! Did he see who she was with?"

"Yes, but it was no one he knew. It was a woman."

"Did he get a good look at her?"

"Not very, apparently. Dark, curly hair, pink dress."

"That's *all*?"

"He's not a real verbal guy. I got the impression he could recognize her again; he just didn't know how to describe her."

"Terrific. If I find her I'll bring her right over for an I.D."

"What are you so down about?"

"Oh, nothing. I mean, I don't want to talk about it. What's the other tidbit you mentioned?"

"I got a threatening phone call. A whispery voice, demanding to know where Lindsay is. I couldn't tell if it was a man or a woman."

"What was the threatening part?"

"It said, 'Where is Lindsay Hearne?' and I said, 'Who is this?' and it said, 'You're next.' So I said, 'What the hell do you mean?' and it said, 'If you want to live, tell me where Lindsay Hearne is.' So I hung up."

"You're kidding."

"No. Why not? I didn't have anything else to say to the creep."

"I mean the whole thing. They guy really said, 'You're next'?"

"I'm not at all sure it was a guy."

"Susanna, for Christ's sake. You aren't taking this seriously?"

"I've gotten a lot of crank calls in my life."

"You've got to tell Blick about this. Promise me." And I told her about my brakes.

In the end, she promised to call Blick and to have her husband pick her up after work for a few days so she wouldn't have to stand at any dark bus stops.

I rang off, feeling not at all relieved. Feeling worse than ever, in fact. I didn't like the sound of that "next" at all. I wondered if Brissette and Tillman had gotten similar calls—Brissette, at least, had gotten some kind of call that summoned him to the staircase. If these calls were a pattern, that meant we were dealing with some kind of crazy. If he threatened to kill people unless they told him where Lindsay was, and then did it, that meant he was nuts.

But the nuts theory didn't explain either Birnbaum's murder or the attempts on me. It was probably about as good as all the other theories I'd had in this case. Useless. Which was how I felt.

I called Joan, half hoping she'd be in distress so I could rescue her. "Are you okay?" I said, as if she'd just lived through a six-car collision.

"Of course. Why wouldn't I be?" She sounded as if she had her own nuts theory.

"There's a weirdo about. Someone assaulted Sardis and Susanna got a threatening call."

"I'm sorry to hear it, Paul, but I don't see what it's got to do with me."

"The weirdo's looking for Lindsay."

"How do you know it's the same person?"

"I don't. But if it's two, that doubles the danger. Don't you see that?"

"What are you trying to say?"

"I just thought maybe you could go away for a few days. After all, Susanna's married and Sardis—" I stopped. I was about to say Sardis had me to protect her, but I remembered it was a secret. "I'll try to get Sardis to go too. Maybe you could stay with a friend."

Joan laughed her crazy laugh. "Paul, it's very sweet of you to be concerned, but I really don't think I have anything to worry about."

A cool customer, that one. "Okay. Whatever you say. Incidentally, did you see Lindsay the night before she left?"

"Incidentally! Incidentally, my ass. Who do you think you are, calling up and giving me that song and dance to soften me up before you ask what you really want to know?"

"Joan, I assure you—"

"How dumb do you think I am, Mr. Hotshot Reporter? I have to deal with people in business every day and I have seen a shabby trick or two in my life. Nobody's more shameless or has less conscience than your average banker—they're so used to lying and cheating they'll tell you it's midnight while the noon whistle's blowing and not even get embarrassed about it. That's just how they operate normally, but in my case they pile it on a little higher because I'm a woman and they think I'm even more gullible than your garden-variety sucker. So I'm used to jerks like you, only a lot more high-powered and smarter. Just what do you think you're trying to pull?"

"I'm not trying to pull anything. I just wondered—"

"You just wondered. Well, you can just wonder some more. It's none of your damned business, anyway."

She hung up.

Of course, if she were the Hunan mystery woman, I hadn't really expected her to tell me so. On the other hand,

I certainly hadn't expected to be compared to every huckster in the sordid circles Joan apparently moved in.

If I'd thought I felt bad before, I was an innocent child. This was shaping up as easily the worst day of my life, and it wasn't nearly over yet. There was only one thing to do.

I looked at my watch. Joey and I had gotten back from lunch at three and it was now approaching four. For most people that's a great time to knock off early, but at the *Chronicle* it was one hour before deadline. It wasn't going to be easy to entice Debbie Hofer to the nearest bar.

That was what I thought, but it wasn't as hard as all that. She was softened up by the time I got to the car, even before I mentioned the outraged Rabbit-owner. By then she was reaching for her coat.

I didn't really want to get drunk, as I was hoping for a cozy evening with Sardis and I didn't want to make a bad impression. I mean, yet another bad impression.

But I drank a few beers and tried not to cry in them as I brought Debbie up to date. Of course, no one in the office was supposed to know what I was working on—that was the rule for special assignments—but Debbie was different. Or another way to put it, the pressure was getting to me.

I thought maybe we'd put our heads together and she'd come up with something. I thought she'd be so upset that somebody was trying to kill one of her favorites that she'd solve the thing even as we talked. In a pig's eye.

Speaking around a cigarette, she nodded and said: "It sounds good. This could be it."

"Could be what, for Christ's sake? This is my life we're talking about."

"Calm down. Nobody's going to kill you. It could be love, fool."

"Debbie, of course it's love. Marry me."

"Hush, I'm thinking. How long have you been staying with Sardis?"

143

"Four days. If you count the night I passed out on her couch."

"Have you had any fights yet?"

"Deb, in case you haven't been listening, my life may be at stake."

"Better yet. That means you're under stress—fights run statistically higher than average under stress conditions. And you can be a brat. I've seen it." Debbie nodded some more, still evaluating. "She sounds good; I'd go for it."

"But—"

"Paul. Stop a minute. How do you really feel about her?"

I didn't answer. I was trying to think.

"Tell your auntie."

I took a deep breath. "She's terrific."

"That's what you think about her. How do you feel?" Another deep breath. "Pretty strongly."

"That's what I thought. It's 4:30 Friday afternoon, May 7, okay? In a month, let's have another chat."

I didn't see what she was getting at. "You've lost me."

"Well, it's this way—I've kind of noticed over the years that you've got sort of a selective memory about certain things. A month from now I'm just going to remind you what you said today. That's all."

"Jesus, Debbie. I was hoping for a little sympathy. And all I'm getting is a lecture on something I don't even understand. You're not making any sense, you know that?"

"I'm just saying be a little extra careful with Sardis; you could blow it real easy."

"I could die real easy, goddammit!"

"Nonsense. If they wanted to kill you, you'd be dead already."

I stopped staring into my glass and stared at Debbie instead. I didn't speak, trying to assimilate what she'd said, but she made it easy for me: "They're trying to scare you off the story, that's all. Think about it. All the guy in the car had to do was make it look like he was trying to run you down. And a Molotov cocktail in your window— come on! The brakes are sillier still, unless you were parked on Mt. Diablo or something."

On reflection, I decided she was right, sort of. If the murderer really wanted to kill me, he'd just do it—like he'd killed Jack and Brissette and Tillman. So Deb was probably right; he proabably was just trying to scare me. But the way he was going about it, I felt he harbored a reckless disregard for my health.

Still, I left Deb feeling somewhat cheered. Somewhat beat my previous cheered level all to hell.

The mood lasted until I got home and found an empty house. I could have called Sardis to see if she was working late, but I felt that would be interfering in her life. I could have made myself an omelet and some home fries. But hell. I was full of afternoon martinis and evening beer. I'd had the worst day of my life, unless you counted the one three days earlier when I woke up and found my house had ceased being a home.

I fed Spot and went to sleep on Sardis' bed.

She shook me awake after a while. "Have you eaten?"

"No. What time is it?"

"Nearly nine. I worked late again." She kissed me.

And all of a sudden I felt the best I'd felt all day. Considering the kind of day it was, I'd better rephrase that—I actually felt good. Like maybe things were going to get better after all.

And they did. Right away.

We had a *very* late supper, but by that time we were all showered and sated. There never was a better omelet or better home fries.

While we ate, I told Sardis the bad news and the bad news. First I told her about the brakes, because it was the worst (technically, the worse, if you care). I tempered the story with Debbie's theory and found it had the same somewhat cheering effect on Sardis that it had on me. And then I ruined her evening a second time by telling her the cops hadn't found Lindsay. Once again we tried to figure out where she was and failed. So we moved on to the mystery woman. Sardis pointed out that even Susanna matched the description. I added that so did Joan. And Marilyn Markham. And if you stretched curly to mean wavy and dark to mean non-blonde, so did Sardis. So did Booker Kessler's pal, Denise.

It was very discouraging.

Sardis kissed me again. She suggested we rest our minds with a nooky break, but I was too wound up. I stayed up awhile after she went to bed, trying to make sense out of any of it. I didn't realize I'd fallen asleep until Spot jumped up in my lap and woke me up.

I set the clock for seven o'clock and climbed into bed beside Sardis.

At 7:05 the next morning, as soon as I thought I could speak, I called Jacob Koehler at home. We make a date for breakfast.

CHAPTER 16

We met at the same Denny's where I'd ordered the burger and walked out with it frying after I got the news about Brissette. There aren't a whole lot of restaurants in Emeryville and whatever Jacob wanted was fine with me. I just hoped nobody recognized me and chucked me out.

Jacob's big shoulders sagged a bit. He seemed diminished, somehow. A very worried man.

He said: "I tried to get you yesterday. There isn't much time, I'm afraid."

I found that a bit on the bewildering side. "I returned your call. I even came out to your office. The receptionist said you weren't there."

"Oh? Well, I went in the back door. Maybe she didn't realize."

"Somebody cut my brake lines while I was waiting for you."

"Oh, no! Not the best of neighborhoods, I'm afraid. I apologize."

The waitress brought coffee and we ordered man-sized breakfasts, both of us.

I waited for Jacob to speak again. I couldn't figure him. Did he really think cutting brake lines was garden-variety vandalism? He might. It would be just like a hotshot scientist not to know how a car works. But there was another possibility—maybe he was using his trademark vagueness to cover up the fact that he nobbled my car himself. The person who did it, I figured, had probably followed me to Kogene from the *Chronicle*. How else would they know what my car looked like? Jacob could easily have done that and then gone in the back door he'd just mentioned. "I've decided," he said at last, "to make a public appeal for information about Terry's whereabouts."

"Let me be sure I understand," I said. "You've decided, after all, to go public with the story of the kidnapping?"

"Yes."

"May I ask what prompted your decision?"

"Time's running out. Terry's very ill, Mr. McDonald." The lines around his mouth were about ten feet deep. "She has an incurable disease."

"Leukemia?"

"Why do you think that? Because it's a well-known childhood killer? It's not, you know. In this country it hits more than twenty thousand adults every year, but only about twenty-five hundred children."

"I didn't really guess it at all. Joan told me."

"Joan?"

"Lindsay's sister."

"Oh, yes, Joan. She would know, of course."

"Inspector Blick thought Lindsay might have taken Terry to an 'alternative' cancer specialist."

Koehler winced. His eyes were so full of pain there didn't seem to be room for more. But when I said that, he looked even more hurt. "I know. I can't believe it." His voice broke and for a moment I panicked. Women crying were bad enough, but a giant Nobel laureate who looked more like a god than a man—that I couldn't handle. Especially not at breakfast.

But Jacob got control of himself and went on. "I don't think she'd do a thing like that."

"She must not have," I said. "The police weren't able to find her at any of the obvious places."

"Oh." Apparently, Blick hadn't bothered to tell him. "Blick said you told him Terry wasn't sick."

He looked embarrassed. "I thought it best at the time."

"How so?"

"Terry doesn't know how sick she is. I mean, she doesn't know she could die. So I—Marilyn and I—thought we shouldn't tell the police." He looked very confused, as if he couldn't quite remember his own reasoning process. "We thought she might find out, somehow."

"But how would she find out?"

"The police might tell her. Just somebody might."

"But if the police didn't think she was sick, they wouldn't have looked for her and her mother at the cancer quack hospitals. And they might have passed up a chance to find her."

"But she wasn't there." Jacob looked almost belligerent. He attacked his eggs instead of me.

"Where do you think she is, then?"

"Mr. McDonald, if I knew that, I wouldn't be talking to you. I wouldn't have hired Jack Birnbaum. I'd have Terry back."

So far that was about the only thing he'd said that made sense. "Okay," I said, "I understand. But if you were afraid the cops were going to tell Terry she has leukemia, why are you telling me for a newspaper article?"

Jacob crashed his coffee cup on the table. Coffee went everywhere. "You can't put that in the story!"

He looked like a cornered lion, I thought. He had the mane and the presence and even the sinews. It was very sad to see such a magnificent beast so distressed.

I help up a hand to placate him. "Okay. I won't. But I thought the reason you told me was because you wanted me to."

"Oh. No. I just wanted you to know why there isn't much time. I have to have her back right away."

"I understand. I'm sure any father would feel that way."

"You *don't* understand. I'm not just any father, don't you see that?"

"Well, of course, I—"

"Terry is perfect. A genetically perfect child. She was meant to be perfect. Lindsay and I created her." The terrible hurt in his eyes was replaced by something bright and excited—the kind of avid glint people get when they start on their favorite subject.

I kept quiet and he kept talking.

"The gene pool is in serious trouble, you know. All the wrong people are reproducing."

"The wrong people?"

"Absolutely. The very people who ought to be eugenically sterilized."

"But who are they, exactly?"

He looked as if he'd never encountered ignorance on such a massive scale. "The genetically inferior. Can't you see that? All the brightest people, the ones who really ought to be reproducing, aren't. They're the very ones who get vasectomies or practice contraception." He banged his fist on the table. "The irony of it! It's incredible, isn't it?"

I nodded. I admit I was stringing him along a little. It was an argument I'd heard before—and not always from arch-conservatives, either. It's amazing the number of otherwise decent people who believe in their own genetic superiority. But somehow I didn't expect it to pop out of Jacob's mouth. I wanted to see how far he'd go, so I pretended this was all virgin turf to me.

"If something isn't done, the next generation won't be

fit to cope with the world they're going to inherit. We must breed a super-race, a race of genetically perfect specimens."

I said, "You're Jewish, aren't you, Dr. Koehler?"

He nodded. "Yes, of course. But the Jews aren't the only ones with good genes. Look at Lindsay. She—"

"That isn't what I was getting at. I was thinking that it was this kind of thinking that got six million Jews killed."

Again he pounded the table. The avid glint turned into a slightly mad one. "Don't you see? Can't you see? That's a perfect example of what I'm talking about. It entirely proves my point. Can't you understand that?"

I spoke softly, hoping to defuse him a little. "I'm afraid you're making a leap I can't quite follow. Maybe there's something wrong with my genes."

Of course there was. He'd forgotten that. He was a genetically superior specimen and sometimes he failed to allow for the poorer caliber of lesser brains.

The realization showed in his face and in his softer, more professorial, and distinctly more condescending voice as he explained: "That's what happens when knowledge and power fall into the wrong hands. There was nothing wrong with Hitler's thesis except for one thing—the Germans are not the super-race. It's that simple."

"Oh. Well, then, who is?"

"I'm not saying they don't have some good genes. Excellent in some areas. But they don't have everything. Imagination, for instance. Creativity. Very lacking there. But excellent physical specimens. Excellent." He shrugged. "Anyway, they got a good idea, and because they didn't have the genetically coded ability to understand it, they wound up destroying some of the very finest genes in all the world. A terrific loss to the pool." He spread his arms at the shoulders, like a professor making a point. "That's what happens when inferior specimens get out of control."

"But who are the superior specimens? I mean, any particular group?"

"Of course not. We need the best traits from all racial and ethnic groups. We need to breed like dogs."

Breed like dogs. That was not the cliché as I knew it. I was still struggling with it when he saw that again he'd failed to make himself clear to an inferior specimen.

"I mean, we need to breed people like we breed dogs," he said. "We need to establish breeds for specific purposes. Why not? We do it not only with dogs, but with other animals as well—cows, horses—why not humans? It's the obvious evolutionary step."

"You mean that if for some reason we needed extremely tall geneticists, we would just cross Kareem Abdul Jabbar with, say, Marilyn?"

I used the example of his own wife deliberately and rather harshly, I thought. It was my experience that people who thought they knew exactly what was right for other people frequently didn't see any reason to apply their panaceas to themselves and their families. But if I wanted to see Jacob trip all over himself explaining why my idea was lousy, I was disappointed.

He looked as if he were finally making progress with a C-minus student. "Exactly! The thing could have all sorts of applications in every area of human endeavor. Do you see that, Mr. McDonald? There is nothing, no job, no chore, no task, no condition, that we couldn't very specifically breed people for."

"Isn't this a bit like *Brave New World*?"

"What?"

"The novel by Aldous Huxley. About the future."

"Never heard of it. Lindsay would know—she's the literary one."

"Lindsay? You mean Marilyn."

"Of course not. When would Marilyn have time to read novels? She's like me. I mean, mentally she's like me. Not
152

nearly so good a physical specimen. Good idea to cross her with a basketball player."

"You mentioned Lindsay as if you were still married to her."

"Lindsay's my mate. Perfect mate. Perfect complement. I looked for her until I found her and then I married her. And we bred." His eyes actually got misty.

"What about Marilyn?"

"Marilyn? What about her?"

"Isn't she your mate now?"

"She's my *wife*. I needed one—mostly for Terry, you know. But how on earth could she be my mate? I could never breed with her. Don't you understand? Marilyn has one of the top scientific minds in the country, but she lacks creativity. And beauty. And athletic ability. How could I possibly breed with her? I wanted a perfect child."

"And Terry is a perfect child?"

"Perfect." He got all misty again. "She was talking at eight months. Eight months, Mr. McDonald! Do you know much about children? Eight months! She could say whole sentences in perfect syntax. I taught her to read when she was three. And math, of course. She takes after me in that respect. She's seven now and she can do calculus. But she takes after Lindsay, too. She had short stories published in children's magazines before she started school—official school, I mean. We taught her at home, of course. Or I did."

I didn't know much about children, but it occurred to me that Terry was probably an unbelievably unhappy little girl, with a stage father like this guy.

"Is she beautiful?" I said.

"A perfect physical specimen. Always at least a head taller than the other kids her age. Way ahead of most kids in how fast she learned to sit up and walk and all that stuff. Extremely superior child. Just like I planned it." He took a breath.

153

"You probably wonder why I do what I do when clearly this is the most important work in the world today—establishing human breeding patterns. I'll let you in on something—I'm not going to be doing it forever."

"No?"

"I had to establish credibility first. I've won one Nobel and I'm going to win another for the work I'm doing now. Count on it. It's a certainty. I had to have those credentials before I could get on with my real work. But I've been working on it all along. I found Lindsay and then we bred and then I started Project Terry."

"Project Terry?"

"That's what I call it. Don't ever say it around Lindsay. She hates it." He shrugged his genetically perfect shoulders. "But she'll have to get used to it, I suppose. That's what I'm going to call the book."

"You're writing a book about your daughter?"

He nodded. "Of course. I've kept detailed notes from the first. I'll publish it sometime in the next five years, when she has the equivalent of a college education, maybe a few stories in the *New Yorker*. Who knows? She may have won her own Nobel by then. I've already got her working with me, you know. By the time she's ten, she'll be an above-average scientist, and a couple of years after that, she'll be top caliber."

"What about her illness?" I didn't see any way to avoid bringing up the subject.

He looked infinitely miserable. He nodded. "Yes. She has . . . the susceptibility. Something went wrong."

"You mean the susceptibility to the disease?"

He nodded again. Unbelievably sad. "Something went wrong. She should be a perfect specimen."

"But surely a susceptibility of leukemia isn't in the genes."

"Officially, science doesn't really know. But suppose it is? Then I've failed. Project Terry is a failure. She isn't a genetically perfect child."

154

As I might have mentioned, reassuring people isn't my greatest talent, but this posed a particular challenge. Here was a guy whose daughter was dying and the thing he seemed upset about was that her dying interfered with his pet theory. What in creation was I supposed to say?

Before I could decide, Jacob started up again. "I have to fix her. That's why it's so important that I find her. Don't you see that?"

I was beginning to. "The work you're doing that you mentioned. Is it a cure for leukemia?"

"Yes, yes, of course. Of course it is. I'm the only one who can help her. The only one in the world." This time the sad eyes overflowed and I was indeed stuck with a crying genius. I pretended it wasn't happening.

"Your cure is ready? I knew Kogene was working on something big, but I didn't realize it was quite this far along."

"It's there. The animal testing is done. We can't market it until we do the human testing—but it works. Of course it works. I'd know, wouldn't I? I'm Jacob Koehler. If I don't know, who does? It works. It's the answer—the smart bomb."

"I beg your pardon?"

"That's how it works—it's a smart bomb."

"I'm afraid you've lost me."

He waved a hand. "It's not important. I doubt you could follow it, anyway."

"You're using it to treat Terry?"

"Of course, McDonald, of course. You don't think I'd deprive my own daughter, do you? The FDA can't come right in a man's home and tell him what to do about his daughter."

"Is she getting better?"

"Certainly." He smiled. "She really is, you know that?" And then he remembered what had happened. "I mean, she was. She's missed two treatments already. That's why

155

you can help me. If I make this public plea and someone has seen her, then I can get her back. Do you see how important it is?"

For such a handsome guy, he could really look pathetic sometimes. Could he really be so attached to an idea that he could get this miserable about it, or did he have some human feeling for his daughter, deep down? I didn't figure now was the time to ask.

"I'll be glad to do what I can, Dr. Koehler. But tell me something. Did Lindsay know you were treating Terry?"

"I haven't seen Lindsay much lately. Usually Marilyn deals with her."

"You didn't tell her about the treatments? After all, she is the child's mother."

"We did talk about it. I remember. We talked about it the last time I saw her—when she brought Terry back."

"That was the first time you talked about it?"

"I think so. Yes. Yes, it was. She asked me a lot of questions about it, as if she hadn't heard of it before. I remember I was surprised I hadn't told her." He smiled again, for the second time in our interview. "I guess I'm a little absentminded."

"Did Terry's doctor know about the treatments?"

"I'm her doctor."

"I mean her pediatrician. She must have gone to one originally, when she first became ill."

"Oh, yes, of course she did. Dr. Morgan Rumler at the medical center. Good doctor."

"Did Dr. Rumler know about the treatments?"

"Of course not. What would be the point?"

"I was just wondering. Let's talk about the news story a little. I presume everything we've said here today is off the record?"

"Definitely. I just want to make an appeal."

"We'll have to explain all about Lindsay and the kidnapping. You understand that, don't you?"

"Why? All we have to do is say if anybody's seen Terry, they should bring her back."

I knew he was going to say that before he said it. I knew it partly because he was a genetic engineer and used to being the smartest guy around. But also because in the newspaper business everybody wants to tell you your job. Everyone knows exactly what should be in a story and what shouldn't. The fact that you've written six or eight newspaper stories every day of your life for the past fifteen years and they've never written one cuts absolutely no ice. They also think that if a newspaper agrees to interview them, they've just been offered a public forum for their ideas or a free ad for their business or a guaranteed press release that'll get them a better job. If the story doesn't come out that way, they get pissed off.

I told Jacob we couldn't tell people to bring Terry home without first saying she was missing and he said he didn't see why not and we went around for a while. That's the way it always is.

Finally he saw that nothing was going to get in the paper unless he gave in a bit, and so he did. That's also the way it always is, and it's very trying, all that wasted energy.

Then I told Jacob I needed a couple of desperate-father quotes to round things out.

"Just tell them," he said, "that I miss her. I'm not myself without her. I need her and miss her and want her back with me."

Now was the time to ask the question that was bothering me. "Do you love her?" I said.

" She's my whole life."

It was about the weirdest breakfast of my life, but at least there was a page 1 story in it. I went back, wrote it, and handed it in. Joey did exactly what I knew he'd do—sent me back to Kogene with a cameraman.

Steve Koehler was in the reception area when we got

there. He walked over and shook hands, all smiles. "Nice to see you again. What can we do for you?"

But I didn't have to answer because Jacob poked his head out about that time, apparently looking for Steve. I told him we needed a picture to go with the story and also mentioned something else Joey wanted—a few quotes from Marilyn.

So he went to get her and it was obvious this was the first she'd heard of the interview. But she gave the quotes and they posed together. They seemed happy. At least they seemed to have some sort of strong bond between them. Probably it was genetics. At any rate, it was hard for me to reconcile the notion of being married to a woman like Marilyn Markham with Jacob's cold dismissal—"*How on earth could she by my mate? How could I possibly breed with her?*"

It was equally hard to reconcile his crazy story about Project Terry with the way he said "She's my whole life." The way he looked and sounded when he said it damn near made me cry.

CHAPTER 17 I went

back to the office and called the University of California Medical Center. They told me Dr. Rumler was in pediatrics at Moffitt Hospital and on vacation. So I called Booker the burglar.

"How'd you like to help me out again tonight?"

"I don't know. How interesting is it?"

"UC Med Center. A doctor's office."

"Not bad." He thought a minute. "A piece of cake, of course, but at least it has a little color to it. What are we looking for?"

"A patient's chart."

"I like it. I wouldn't mind at all."

"What time do we go?"

"I can't tell yet. I've got some arrangements to make. Can you call back in two hours?"

"Sure."

159

Next I called John Reid, the young biochemist who'd shown me around Kogene.

"Have you ever heard of something called a smart bomb?"

"Sure. It's a way of delivering a drug to the target site."

"Come again?"

"Say the disease is—oh, breast cancer—and you've got a cure for it. You've still got to get it to the afflicted cells—they're the target site."

"Go on."

"So, say breast cancer manifests a protein that distinguishes it from healthy cells—let's call that Protein B. You can use antibodies to recognize it."

"How's that?"

"A monoclonal antibody is one that will bind to only one thing. So if you can find the one that binds to Protein B, you can make a smart bomb and zap the cancer."

"Oh. So how do I do it?"

"Well, you just mix your drug with your antibody and a lipid and you pass sound through it. Then what happens is like a miracle. Everything assembles into a biological form called a micelle—a little cell with the drug in it. The antibody is embedded in the lipid, and it sticks out, so it can bind with the protein. It's like one of those oranges stuck with cloves."

I thanked him and hung up.

It was late enough to have a beer and go home and I did, hoping I wasn't going to find an empty house again. I kind of liked having Sardis around.

She was there all right, with a pork roast in the oven and a pie cooling on top of the fridge. She all but met me at the door with a martini. She had on a dress and her legs looked terrific. She was terrific. Spot was terrific. It was all terrific. I wondered if this was what it was like to have a family.

We had some Mondavi Barberone. Sardis kicked off her

shoes and sat at the end of the sofa with her feet in my lap. We had some more Barberone.

Eventually Sardis took her feet out of my lap and sat in it herself and wrapped her gorgeous legs around me and kissed me. I kissed her back. Her fingers made little feathery strokes on my back and neck and face.

All very nice, but I just wasn't in the mood to go any further. I stopped kissing her and just sort of held her, hoping she'd get the idea. She did, but she wanted things absolutely clear: "Don't you want to make love?"

"Not right now. Maybe later."

"Is something bothering you?"

"No. Not really. I have to go out for a while tonight. I guess I'm not very relaxed."

She looked at her watch. "When do you have to go?"

"Omigod. I have to make a phone call." I was an hour late calling Booker.

He said we had to be at the hospital before eight, because that was when visiting hours ended. He also told me what to wear and pointed out that it was after seven. So much for the pork roast.

"Bad news," I told Sardis. "I have to go now."

"When will you be back?"

"With any luck, around ten or eleven, I'd say. Maybe later."

"But you haven't eaten."

I kissed her lightly. "A fact I very much regret. I'm really sorry about this."

"Maybe I could make you a sandwich."

"No, thanks. Listen, I've got to change." I went in the bedroom and put on my new white jeans and an ordinary button-down pinstripe shirt, as Booker had ordered. (Actually, he said to make sure the shirt was a few years old and a little frayed, but the only clothes I had were brand-new. It was just dumb luck I'd bought white jeans instead of tan ones.)

"You look very nice," Sardis said. "Do you think . . . I mean, would it be all right if I asked you where you're going?"

"I'm sorry," I said. "I can't tell you."

"Oh. I guess I made an ass of myself making dinner and everything. I forgot you had a social life before I knew you."

"Look, I can't talk about it now. I'm late."

"Maybe when you come home."

"There's something I ought to tell you. I may not make it home tonight." I meant, of course, that I might be arrested, but in retrospect I have to admit the timing was terrible. Sardis looked stricken, so I said, "Will you bail me out if I don't?"

She managed only a very pallid little smile, thinking I was making a joke to cover an awkward moment. But there was no time to deal with it now. I had to go burgle a hospital.

Booker and I met outside our target. He was wearing a white jacket, the sort you can buy at any uniform supply store, and jeans. He pulled a stethoscope out of his pocket and told me to put it around my neck. I did and we looked exactly like a couple of hip young docs.

There was a candy stand to the left as we entered, and an information desk on the right. Near the candy stand was a hospital directory. Booker never gave it a glance. He just sauntered, bearing left, till he got to the elevators. I followed him aboard and he punched 8.

We couldn't talk as we rode, as we weren't alone, but when we got off, Booker sauntered us unerringly to a men's room. No one was there, and a good thing, because I could hardly contain my enthusiasm for Booker's style: "Those 'arrangements' you mentioned. You cased the joint."

He shrugged. "It's my job."

"Did you buy the stethoscope especially for this?"

"No. It kind of comes in handy sometimes in my work. But the jacket's new—you like?"

"You can wear it to Perry's."

"No, no, no. McDonald, you don't know anything. It's for Carlos O'Brien's in Triburon."

"Oh." An amazing man, Booker. A key for every lock and the right clothes for every singles joint.

"Now, here's the drill. I don't know what security is like after eight o'clock, but I figure as long as we look like docs we can pretty much come and go as we please. It's 7:50 now. Take off your stethoscope."

I did and he took off his coat. Now I was just a visitor in white jeans and Booker was another in regular jeans. "Let's go in the meditation room until just before eight— they may lock it for the night—and then we'll go down to six."

"Six?"

"The sixth floor. Pediatrics."

The meditation room had ornate wooden doors that looked as if, in less secular days, they'd opened into a chapel. The room itself was bare and a bit grim. Booker pulled a couple of straight wooden chairs close to the wall and sat down in one, facing the wall and keeping his back very straight. I sat in the other and followed suit.

We were alone in the room, but if someone came in, all he'd see would be the backs of two serious meditators, probably with desperately ill family in the hospital. Probably he'd leave right away, embarrassed at disturbing us. Booker had thought of everything.

At 7:59 exactly, Booker got up, motioned for me to follow, and led the way back to the men's room. Again, no one was there, so we slipped into our respective stetho-scope and coat and stepped back into the corridor.

The next part was an unbelievable piece of cake. We just got off the elevator, turned right, and went through a door

163

that led to a corridor with eight or ten doctors' offices opening off it. Booker was a marvel.

It was nothing to find Dr. Rumler's office and walk right in, with the aid of the key of the day, selected by Booker in about one and one half seconds. Dr. Rumler had a file cabinet and three deep drawers in his desk. Terry Koehler's chart wasn't in it or them.

"It's a bust," I said.

"Can't find it?" Booker's voice was sympathetic. "Is the chart you want the only one missing? Or aren't there any charts at all here?"

"No charts at all."

"Well, never fear. They must be somewhere in the hospital. The question is where."

"Maybe we could just walk to the pediatrics desk and ask for it."

Booker shook his head. "Too risky. The nurse or whoever's there must know what docs would be on at night. We can only get away with this if people see us at a distance. I mean, we look like we might be docs or we might be orderlies or even male nurses, I guess. But we don't know who's authorized to look at a chart and who's not."

"What do you think we should do?"

"Let's just take a spin around and see what we can see."

"Okay."

We walked down the corridor with the offices and turned onto another full of rooms with sick kids in them. The light was dim and I thought it was one of the most depressing places I'd ever been. But then we came to a more depressing one—the corridor with the intensive care nursery on it. You could see the babies through the windows—most of them about the size of a football and lots of them full of tubes and needles. At the moment I wasn't crazy about Booker's job.

We passed the desk and saw a rack full of blue loose-leaf

notebooks that looked like charts for the patients who were currently admitted. What we didn't see was a sort of central room where old charts were kept.

We found yet another corridor—the floor's main one—and gave it a whirl. It, too, housed a lot of doctor's offices, but it also had doors with no names on them. Booker simply opened them up. But not a chart did we find.

"That must mean," Booker said, "that all the hospital's charts are kept together, rather than separately by clinic. Maybe even all the charts from all the hospitals in the med center are kept together."

"We've got to find out where."

"I've got an idea. Let's go back to Rumler's office."

Booker's idea was simplicity itself. He picked up Rumler's blue med center directory and turned to Charts. That didn't work, so he tried Records. No luck, but he was undaunted. He simply started at the beginning and read every listing, looking for a likely one. Fortunately, he only had to go halfway through the book: Medical Records had to be it.

The only trouble was, the directory didn't say where it was. All it had in it were phone numbers, not locations. Clearly we couldn't ask someone in the hospital, as we were supposed to look like we knew what we were doing. Even if we got away with it, it would draw attention to us. So that was out. At least that was my theory.

"*Au contraire*," said Booker. "Asking someone in the hospital is the only way to find it. Ergo, exactly what we shall do." He talked funny for a burglar.

But he burgled like an angel. He motioned me to follow him to the first floor, where he found a pay phone and dialed Moffitt Hospital.

"Hello," he said, "can you tell me where Medical Records is?"

The operator said something, probably, "Shall I connect you?"

"No, thanks," said Booker. "A friend who works there left something at my house and I need to return it. . . . Okay, good. Where's that, exactly? Got it. Thanks a lot."

He got off the phone, giggling his head off. "Everybody's so goddam helpful. I could have called my friend, right? And asked him where his office is. But she was so busy being nice she didn't even think of it. Sort of restores your faith in human nature, being a crook."

"I wouldn't have thought of it exactly that way."

Booker nodded. "It's true though. There'd be a lot less crime today if the average citizen were more suspicious."

"So where's Medical Records?"

"Let's sit down a minute." He led the way to a batch of chairs near the doors. "Here's the thing. It's not in this building. It's in the Ambulatory Care Center, that big glass building across the street."

"Let's go."

"Uh-uh. I haven't cased it. There might be a security guard or God knows what kind of alarm system. There might even be people working in the building. Anyway, I have a funny feeling about Medical Records."

"What?"

"Well, listen, if you had some chronic disease and you were in and out of the hospital, sometimes you might get sick at night, right? And they'd need your chart."

"So you think Medical Records is open all night. I mean twenty-four hours a day. Unburgleable."

"Nothing is unburgleable."

"I don't see any lights over there."

"Means nothing. The record room could be in the back of the building."

"So what do we do?"

"I'm thinking."

I let him think.

He sighed, finally. "If it were daytime, I'd just go over and have a look. It's got to be done tonight?"

"Should have been done last night."

"We need an inside source. You don't know any medical librarians, do you?"

"God, no. Wait a minute!" I said the two sentences back-to-back, falling all over each other, concurrently practically. Inspiration had come with the speed of light. "Erin Harris."

"You do know one."

"Not exactly. She used to work for the New York City Public Library."

"Terrific."

"Hang on a second. She forsook it all to move here. Now she's in the clerical pool at the med center. I think she got sick of cataloguing."

Booker brightened. "How well do you know her?"

"Well enough. She knows I write mysteries. I'll just say I need help with a plot."

"You better hope she's home."

She was. And eager to help, like the hospital operator. From Erin I learned these important facts: Medical Records was indeed open twenty-four hours a day; if a doctor needed a file at night, a messenger was sent for it; it was completely computerized and you needed the number of a chart to get the chart.

I also learned it was in the basement and there was a side entrance on the plaza outside the building. I wasn't sure what that meant, but I figured it would come clear once we got down to serious burgling.

So it looked like all we had to do was call up, claim to be Dr. Rumler, than go across the street and claim to be a messenger and we'd have one Terry Koehler hospital chart in our possession. If we could get its number, somehow.

That meant a wholesale search of Rumler's office. And that meant going back to the sixth floor. So we did.

I'm sure Rumler must have had some system for keeping chart numbers—exactly what we wanted must have been somewhere in that office—but neither I nor the best little burglar in the West could turn it up.

Ingenuity was called for. I turned to Booker.

"Only one thing to do," he said. "Invoke Kessler's Fourth Law of Burglary."

"Great idea. What is it?"

"When in doubt, brazen it out."

"You mean storm the building?"

"Nope. Call Medical Records, say you're Rumler and don't have the number for some reason or other."

"You're the doctor."

"No, you are." He pushed the phone at me and I dialed Medical Records.

"This is Dr. Rumler," I said, "and—"

"Dr. Rumler!" It was a light male voice. "You sound awful!"

"I . . . well. I probably shouldn't be working, but—"

"You certainly shouldn't. You're exposing the patients. You should go right home and have Georgie feed you some chicken soup. In fact, I've got half a mind to call him right now to come get you."

Now I don't like stereotypes any better then the next person, but I deduced from this chap's voice and prissy manner of speech that he was of the homosexual persuasion. (Believe me, I don't think all gays are prissy, but this guy was femme. Or whatever they call it.) And from the way he was carrying on about Georgie, I figured Rumler was too. Probably had a wimpy voice like this character's.

So I started speaking in a cracked half-whisper, like I really did have a cold. "Believe me, I'd be home if I could. I've got an emergency. I've got my hands pretty full and don't have time to look up the chart number."

"What's the name? I'll feed it to the computer."

"Terry Koehler."

A moment passed and then he said, "Got it."

"I'll send someone right over. It'll be a new guy."

"Okay, Doc. You take care of that cold now."

I hung up. "It worked."

"Of course it worked. Booker the Burglar always comes through."

Booker looked more the messenger type than I did, so we decided he should make the pickup.

Per Erin's directions, we went to the left side of Ambulatory Care, where, surrounded by dense evergreens, we found a stairway leading down from the sidewalk to the plaza Erin mentioned.

And that plaza, let me tell you, was something to see. The med center was on top of a hill on a street called Parnassus, and so the plaza, even though it was on the basement floor of the building next door and ten or twelve feet below the sidewalk, was a steep cliff at the other end. It had a banister around it, being an urban cliff, but it was still a wild and spectacular thing. It showed you all the lights of the city, and some across the bay as well.

Mesmerized, I walked back to the banister, Booker following. For the moment I'd forgotten the serious work of burgling and I honestly believe he had too. That plaza was something else.

But there's only so long you can look at lights, so in a few minutes we ambled back to Ambulatory Care. Booker went up to the glass door and knocked or rang a bell or something, and I stayed a few feet away, just out of sight, still staring at the view.

Somebody came to the door, and I barely paid attention to what happened next, I had so much faith in Booker. But to the best of my recollection, there was an exchange something like this:

"Hi. I'm here to pick up Terry Koehler's chart. For Dr. Rumler."

"Poor Dr. Rumler! What a time for an emergency."

"He'll be all right. I think he sounds worse than he feels."

169

For some reason, I turned in their direction then, and what I saw was not reassuring. The medical librarian looked terrified. He tried to push the door shut.

But Booker had his foot in it. He grabbed for the chart, but the librarian, a split second ahead of him, jerked it out of his way, turned tail, and started running down the corridor.

"Let's go," Booker hollered, and opened the door a little wider.

I followed him into Ambulatory Care, no longer ambling at all. I hadn't figured out what scared the librarian; I just knew he was moving fast.

That basement floor was as spooky a place as you'd want to be in the middle of the night while committing a felony. Mostly, its walls were a sort of dull orange, which wasn't the spooky part, but the orange sections alternated with big hunks of aggregate concrete, which was. These concrete parts kind of stuck out—maybe they were meant to resemble half-pillars or something, but the effect was more cave like than classically elegant.

As he ran, the librarian hollered: "Help! Joe! Joseph! Call the cops!" So clearly the thing to do was to get to Joe.

The librarian was in the lead; Booker was gaining on him, and I was gaining on both of them when I passed a door with a window in it and happened to glance in. What I saw was a room with bookshelves to the ceiling, arranged like stacks in a library and jammed with manila file folders. A vast, cavernous room. Near the door were a few tables, and seated at one of them was a young man dialing a telephone. I surmised that this, at last, was the long-sought Medical Records. I also surmised that if I didn't get my ass in there fast, it was going to get thrown in the Big House.

I didn't want to add assault to my crimes, so I figured the best approach was the lightning instilling of fear. You and I know I'm gentle as a gerbil, but I look a lot more like a bear and Joe there might have been the guy I talked to on the phone—he had the body to go with the voice. I crashed through the door, raised my arms in an ersatz karate pose, jumped up in the air, and yelled, "EEEEEEEyah!"

Instantly Joe quit dialing. I was beginning to think there was something to this genetic superiority after all.

But then Joe stood up, bent his knees, and arranged his arms in a karate pose that didn't look ersatz worth a damn. I backed up a step and he came forward one. I figured backing up was very poor policy if I was planning to instill fear in this runt, but going forward seemed an even worse idea. Joe moved his arms in an entirely menacing manner while I tried to think what to do next.

And then the door opened very suddenly indeed. The first librarian, still clutching the file, came through as if pursued by killer bees. Booker came through right after him.

They ran between Joe and me and I started chasing them, hoping Joe would forget about the phone in the thrill of the moment. He did. It was probably the triumph of his life, terrifying a man-mountain such as myself. He joined the parade, hollering a bunch of karate-sounding stuff.

For the moment I wasn't being torn limb from limb by some kid half my size, nor was I being reported to the authorities, so I should have been happy. But it occurred to me there was something wrong with this picture—how was I ever going to get the file and get out of there if I was being chased? I pondered the problem as I ran down one row of stacks and up the next. Something had to break soon.

It did, of course. The first librarian and Booker got so far ahead that they were in a separate row when the librarian banged into one of the stacks and knocked it over

171

backward—right onto my Atlas-like shoulders. If it had been full of books I'd have been buried alive. But manila folders were nothing much. Most of them slid onto the floor and the ones that were left were nothing I couldn't handle, but I couldn't seem to get the thing righted. So there I was with a bookcase on my back. Being smaller, Joe escaped scot-free from the avalanche, but was he grateful that I'd probably saved his life by taking the blow? Hah! He punched me in the stomach.

Then there was an awful crash from the next row over, an *oof* noise and a beleaguered, librarian-sounding squeal. I figured Booker had finally caught the other guy. So did Joe. He landed another one in my stomach, then squeezed past me, to lend his expertise in the martial arts.

I had to get the damn bookcase off my back; there were no two ways about it. I gave a mighty heave, backward. It worked. Unfortunately, I understimated my heaving ability.

The bookcase went as far as it could, crashing into the next bookcase and starting a chain reaction that brought down the next three stacks as well. Booker and the librarians were buried alive.

But fortunately they were buried under only one bookcase, and an empty one at that. All I had to do was pick it up and they'd be rescued.

"Partner," I said (not wanting to use Booker's name), "you okay?"

"I've got him," said Booker.

"How about you, Joe?"

No answer.

"Okay, Joe, listen. I've got a gun. I'm going to hold it in my hand while I lift the bookcase. It's going to be kind of awkward, and if I'm not careful, the gun might go off and you never know who might get hurt. So I'm not going to need any distractions, okay?"

172

No answer. I figured I hadn't fooled Joe for a second. But I couldn't stand there all night with Booker buried under the bookcase. I lifted it off.

And sure enough, Joe lunged the instant he was free. I turned to face him—God, he was coming right at me—and not knowing what else to do, I ducked.

Since I didn't know karate and had no idea what Joe was up to, I couldn't have predicted the result and I'm still not sure exactly how it happened. But I think Joe simply zigged where I expected him to zag and that's how my head, coming down fast and scared, happened to catch him full in the chest and knock the wind out of him. Maybe he didn't really know karate after all.

Anyway, now I had committed assault, whether I meant to or not. I didn't know much about assault etiquette, so I had to make do with a combination of common decency and tough-guyness—meaning I asked him if he was all right and helped him get up, just like anyone would, only I had to hold both his wrists while doing it, to make sure he didn't try something fancy.

Booker was holding the other guy's wrists behind his back. "Where's the file?" I said.

"I've got it. I mean, I think I can find it. Skinny here dropped it when I tackled him."

"Skinny! Look who's talking," said Skinny.

"Shut up, Skinny," said Booker. To me, he said, "We've gotta tie these guys up."

"Hey, listen," said Joe. "We won't call the cops. I mean, not right away. Just take the file and go and we'll give you fifteen minutes."

"Yeah, you will like my partner's got a gun," said Booker. "Take off your shirt."

"Take off your shirt," I said to Joe, dropping one of his wrists to make it possible.

We sat them in chairs, back to back, and tied them together with their own shirts and belts, poor bastards.

While Booker was getting the file, I asked Skinny a question: "What tipped you off my partner wasn't sent by Dr. Rumler?"

"The pronoun," he said.

"Huh?"

"Rumler's a woman."

CHAPTER 18

We stopped at a phone booth a few blocks away, called the hospital, and told them to check their librarians. It was the least we could do—to this day I feel bad about tying those guys up and wrecking their library.

Then we went to Booker's place and looked at the file. It was the first time I'd been in his apartment and all I can say is, the burgling business must be good. Booker has one of the more impressive art collections I have seen in a private home. Anyway, we looked at the file.

It said Dr. Rumler had seen Terry on the Saturday before she disappeared. Saturday. The day docs play tennis and sail their sloops. I checked to see if Rumler had seen Terry on other Saturdays. She hadn't. Which meant, I thought, that Lindsay had convinced her it was an emergency. That fit with Jacob's saying he and Lindsay had talked about his treatments the last time Lindsay brought Terry back. I figured what happened was that

175

Terry had mentioned the treatments and Lindsay had taken her to Rumler to have her checked out.

As far as I could make out from the file, she was in remission—but she was going blind. And that wasn't all. She was jaundiced. It looked as if Jacob's bomb wasn't as smart as he thought. The doctor had noted "poss. side effs."

I figured Jacob had lied to me. Lindsay must have done a good deal more than ask him a lot of questions about his treatments. She'd probably told him to stop them.

And he must have refused and that was why she snatched the kid. She was afraid the treatments were actually hurting Terry, that they were causing her to go blind and destroying her liver. She was afraid Jacob was so wrought up about Terry that he'd lost his judgment—couldn't tell if something was bad for her or not; wanted to think he could cure her and wouldn't look at the facts or listen to anybody else. That must have been what went through her mind when she made the snatch.

But where the hell had she taken the kid? I didn't have a clue.

I took myself home and to bed. By home, I mean to Sardis', and by bed, I mean the sofa. I didn't think about where I was going to sleep; I just sort of automatically went to the sofa. For some reason I didn't feel like sleeping with Sardis.

It didn't occur to me to wonder what the reason might be until I was just drifting off. I had some passing sort of erotic fantasy and remembered we'd been having a terrific time together. In bed especially. So why the hell did I suddenly out of the clear blue not feel like sleeping with her? It struck me as odd. She'd probably been disappointing me in some way I couldn't quite put my finger on. She'd acted possessive before I went out—maybe that was it.

It must be. I was feeling crowded or something. Or she

wasn't going to work out and I was starting to see it. That's just the way things are sometimes.

The smell of coffee woke me up. I went in the kitchen to get some, but Sardis hadn't made enough for me. She said she didn't know how long I wanted to sleep. She didn't say much else, and neither did I.

I made my own coffee while she read the *Chronicle*, the business section. Then I remembered I had a story in the paper, for the first time in two years. I picked up the front section to find Jacob and Marilyn staring at me from page 1. My very own byline lent authority to a story headlined: BIZARRE KIDNAP CASE—NOBEL LAUREATE AND TV PERSONALITY. I was actually excited, just like I used to be when I had a page 1 story. Journalism's a dirty job and all that, but it has its cheap little thrills.

"Hey, Sardis," I said, "did you see my story?"

She nodded. "I couldn't miss it, could I?"

"Well?" Journalists are like two-year-old children. They have to be patted on the head and told "good boy" every time they go to the bathroom. I was looking for a pat. She wasn't giving it:

"Well what?"

"What do you think?"

She shrugged. "It was okay."

She got up and left for work.

The average person might have spent five minutes or so staring into space and dwelling on his hurt feelings, but I have excellent powers of concentration. I simply turned to the comics section, read *Doonesbury*, *Gordo*, and *Fred Bassett*. My attention probably wouldn't have strayed throughout a reading of the whole paper, but we'll never know. A ringing telephone interrupted this John Wayne-like project.

It was Susanna Flores: "Paul? We've got an I.D. on the mystery woman."

So caught up was I in "Letters to the Editor" that I

177

temporarily forgot what mystery woman we were talking about. "Umph?" I said. "Umph. Yes. The woman Lindsay met at the Hunan."

"It was Marilyn Markham. The cameraman saw her picture this morning. Good piece, by the way."

"Oh. Thanks." Good heavens. The hoped-for pat on the head. "He's sure it was Markham?"

"Quite sure."

"Good. How are you, by the way? Any more threatening calls?"

"No, thank God. Everything seems fine."

I rang off, phoned Marilyn at Kogene, and asked her how she liked the story. I couldn't resist the opportunity for another pat. But it wasn't forthcoming.

"It was . . . fine," she said, in the brave, reluctant tone you might use if your hostess asked how you'd liked your brains and capers.

All right, then. If she was going to be brutal, so was I. "Did you tell the cops," I said, "that you saw Lindsay the night before she disappeared?"

"What are you talking about?"

"I think they'd be interested," I said.

"What is this? Some kind of blackmail attempt?"

"Dr. Markham, please." I can be very haughty when I don't get my pats. "I think we both want the same thing. Maybe we can work together."

"What do *you* want?"

"To find Lindsay Hearne, of course. Don't you?"

She sucked in her breath. "Yes. Of course."

"I'd like to talk to you about your meeting with her. I don't know how to say this exactly, but I think we should talk alone. I mean—" I meant outside Jacob's presence, but I didn't have to say so. She interrupted me, sounding resigned.

"I suppose we should. Can you come here at seven P.M.?

178

I'll say I'm working late and send Jacob home to make dinner."

"I'll be there."

I didn't have much to do all day. I figured to go into the office and see if I could collect a few more pats, but other than that I was a bit at loose ends. So I sat around the kitchen awhile and had some more coffee and made myself a bagel. I was feeling kind of tense and I didn't know quite why.

Sardis called around eleven. "I'm sorry I was a bitch this morning."

"You weren't a bitch. A couple of months at charm school'd probably fix you right up."

Silence.

"Sardis? Hey, Sardis? Little joke. Honest."

More silence.

"Listen, you weren't a bitch, really. It's nice of you to call."

"I thought your story was good." Her voice sounded all teary.

"You did? Hey, forget charm school. Listen, want to run for president? I'll vote for you, and I think my mother will and I have this friend named Debbie Hofer who might . . ."

"Coming home for dinner? We could have cold pork roast."

"Could we make it late?" I told her about my date with the mystery woman and we agreed to have dinner afterward.

Things were okay between us again. Or so I imagined. I may have mentioned that I make it a point not to think about things I don't want to think about.

I went out, photocopied Terry Koehler's hospital file, bought a manila envelope for the original, and mailed it back to Moffitt Hospital. I wanted to be rid of the thing before I went into the office because I had a feeling there was going to be a police beat story about a certain burglary that Joey was going to ask me some questions about. I was going to have to compound all my other sins by lying to my city editor.

I went in and got that out of the way ("Who, me, Boss? Oh, come on. How could you even think . . ."), wrote a few fan letters to my favorite detective novelists, did a few pages of my own book, and generally passed a pleasant day. I turned up at Kogene at precisely 7:00 P.M.

Marilyn saw me in the reception room, not even in her office. Her demeanor wasn't what you'd call welcoming. In fact, she reminded me of the sculpture in front of the Bank of America building—the one nicknamed "The Banker's Heart". It's the biggest, blackest, hardest rock in the Western Hemisphere.

"I agreed to see you," she said, "because I thought you could do us a lot of harm if I didn't. I never underestimate the power of the press." She spoke bitterly. That kind of hatred and suspicion was one of the reasons I quit journalism.

"But I want you to know," she continued, "that I consider talking about poor Lindsay to be revealing family secrets. I don't think that anything I'm going to tell you could be of any possible journalistic interest and I ask that it be considered off the record. Do you agree?"

"Absolutely."

"All right. What can I do for you?"

"You can tell me what you and Lindsay talked about that Friday."

"Jacob told you about Terry's illness, didn't he?"

"Yes."

"Lindsay was very upset. I mean *extremely* upset, Mr. McDonald. As I said, I don't like talking about family secrets, but I was frankly worried about her. She said the pressure of Terry's illness was getting to her, that she needed time off.

"She said she was having headaches and couldn't think straight. She was planning to take a leave from work. So what she wanted me to do was intercede for her with Jacob—she wanted me to persuade him to let Terry spend some time with her, to let her take Terry to Disneyland, things like that—just to be with her."

"What did you say to her?"

"Frankly, I was very worried about her stability. I said that of course I'd intervene, but that maybe now wasn't the best time, that maybe she should think about getting professional help."

"You mean see a shrink."

Marilyn looked very pained, as if such a thing couldn't possibly happen in the Koehler family, even to its ex-members. "I really thought it had come to that."

"What was her reaction to the suggestion?"

"She got very defensive. I guess that should have been a clue, but I honestly didn't realize things were as bad as they obviously were—I mean, I had no idea she'd kidnap Terry, or I'd never have let her pick her up." She paused, as if reflecting, blaming herself a bit. Then she said, "You won't tell Jacob any of this, will you? I don't want him to know how bad Lindsay's condition actually is. You can understand that, can't you? He's under a lot of strain, and nothing would be served by increasing it."

I didn't answer her. I said, "Did Lindsay mention anything about Jacob's treatments?"

"What treatments?" Her face went white.

"His treatments for Terry's leukemia. Isn't that what you're working on here—a leukemia cure?"

"I can't answer that. But Jacob certainly isn't treating Terry. Where on earth did you get that idea?"

CHAPTER 19

"Just a guess," I said. Jacob had said "off the record," and I always take that to mean *"entre nous."* If he hadn't told his wife, who was I to interfere?

"A bad guess," she said. She had recovered her equilibrium, but I thought I'd given her a shock.

I said I supposed so and I thanked her for her help.

Even though I had a date with Sardis, I drove back slowly, trying to figure things out. Marilyn thought Lindsay was crazy. Even Lindsay's close friends hadn't been too sure about her stability during the last few months. So maybe she was crazy. But what was crazy, anyway? Jacob wasn't what you call your shining example of radiant mental health, and Joan was a little bonkers and Sardis was delightfully neurotic and then there was me. How much crazier could Lindsay be than any of us?

And what, specifically, was Marilyn afraid of? She didn't want Jacob to know how bad Lindsay's condition was, but what difference did it make, really? If she hadn't taken Terry to a cancer quack, what did Jacob have to worry about? Hell, he was a cancer quack himself, and now Marilyn knew it if she hadn't known it before. What did she think Lindsay might do that could be so terrible?

I was thinking so hard about all this I was practically creeping across the Bay Bridge, but no one seemed to care much. I had nearly the whole bridge to myself.

Perhaps Lindsay had some history of mistreating Terry. After all, she hadn't wanted children in the first place, and she'd apparently given up custody without a peep. But maybe it hadn't been exactly that way. Maybe Lindsay had tried to get custody but couldn't. Maybe she was an abusive parent and Jacob could prove it. Yet at one time they'd had joint custody.

I decided that meant nothing—Lindsay could have become abusive during that period. On the other hand, abusive parents, as I understood it, were usually ornery only when their kids got on their nerves. Lindsay was an intelligent woman, however crazy. If Terry was getting on her nerves and she was knocking her around, she'd have enough sense to minimize her time with the kid. Especially if Terry were sick. She especially wouldn't want to lose control now.

On yet another hand, she wouldn't want Jacob giving her a worthless cancer cure with side effects. Maybe she felt she had no choice except to get Terry away and hope she stayed on her own good behavior.

But if she were as unstable as Marilyn said she was, the chances of that were minuscule. So that might be what Jacob would have to worry about if he knew, in Marilyn's words, "how bad Lindsay's condition actually was."

It was a thought, anyway. Did it help in figuring out where the two of them were?

I was mulling that when I noticed a car behind me. I was going about forty-five, and as I may have mentioned, 184 there was hardly anybody else on the bridge. There were several lanes open and anybody could whiz along as fast as he wanted.

So there shouldn't have been a car behind me. But there was; and the odd thing was, it wasn't a small, light-colored car.

Paul, my boy, I told myself, you're the one in bad condition. You're so used to being followed and threatened, you think every time a medium-sized dark car is out for a leisurely drive across the bridge, it must be up to something. A particularly dumb idea when the car that tried to hit you is known to be small and light.

I'll speed up, I thought, and when the other car doesn't, I'll know it isn't tailing me. Up I sped.

For a while the other car continued its snail's pace, but when I really started to move out and put some distance between us, it started speeding up too. Gradually, fairly unobtrusively, but unmistakably.

The Broadway exit was the fastest way to Sardis' and far the most direct, but I whizzed past it and got off at Fifth. I was hoping to maneuver fast enough to confuse the medium-sized dark car and make it miss the exit. But I failed. When I stopped for the light, I saw that it was four or five cars behind me. I couldn't tell if the driver was male or female and I couldn't tell any more about the make, model, and color of the car than I already knew.

I turned right onto Fifth Street and then right onto Mission. The car was still on my tail. I figured I'd better come up with a strategy pretty quick. I passed Fourth Street and then Third. I could always go to First and get back on the bridge, going in the opposite direction. But that would be dumb.

Okay, then, Bozo, said I to myself, what would be smart? I was glad I asked. It came to me in a blinding flash.

The Hall of Justice, which housed Southern Police Station, was only blocks away, at Eighth and Bryant. I had this assassin on my tail who expected me to lead him to the fair Sardis, or merely perhaps to a dark alley where he could garrotte me. Wouldn't he be amazed to wind up at the Hall instead? Even in my pursued state I got a chuckle out of it.

I turned right on Second and then right on Howard, just to make it interesting. After all, this was a chase, right? It might as well be fun. I flew down Howard to Fourth, down Fourth to Folsom, past Folsom because it was one-way, and turned right onto Harrison.

To my delight, the dark car took the bait. It careened after me, not even bothering to disguise its purpose. I sped down Harrison toward Eighth, turned left and then left again on Bryant. The other car was right behind me.

I considered just slamming on the brakes in front of the Hall and getting out and standing there, looking menacing. The idea had a lot of merit. No one would shoot you or run you down in front of a police station, for one thing. For another, there'd be a real macho satisfaction in it. And for a third, I'd almost certainly find out who was trying to kill me.

But it seemed anticlimactic, somehow. This was my first high-speed chase and I wasn't yet ready for it to be over. I wanted about half a dozen more cheap thrills before I went back to my humdrum life.

So I kept going past the Hall and turned into the little street at its side. From my days as a police reporter, I knew it would lead to something really terrific—an entrance to the Hall's underground garage, where cops and public officials parked. Maybe the dark car would chase me around in there, all around between rows of black-and-whites; maybe we'd even crash into a few and I'd get my first demolition derby all rolled up with my first high-speed chase.

You may wonder how I could be calm—playful even—with a homicidal maniac on my tail. Two reasons, I think.

One was that I really did feel safe knowing there were cops all over the block. Another was that I sort of felt I was on the offensive, which I'd never been before with this particular maniac.

Anyway, I turned into that little street, planning to turn again into the underground garage. But a patrol wagon was bearing down on me, more on my side than his and I mean this was a *little* street. I was a split second from a head-on collision.

The cop in the wagon hit his horn, but I don't know what good he thought that would do. There was no time to back up, and anyway, the dark car was right behind me.

I guess he was just letting off steam, because thank God, he climbed the curb on his side and hit the sidewalk. I did the same on mine, whipped past him, hurtled past the guard at the garage entrance, and sailed into the garage, all triumphant.

The only problem was, my follower didn't follow. He whipped around the wagon the same as I did, but he had enough sense not to trap himself in a cul-de-sac. He kept going, while about half the San Francisco police force converged on me. When I shake a tail, I do it with panache.

I'd like to have gotten out of my car and bowed with a flourish, but under the circumstances, there was nothing to do but stick-'em-up like a common societal menace. Because the converging cops all had their guns drawn.

The next few minutes went something like this:

"Uh, you see, fellows, somebody's been trying to kill me and there was this guy tailing me and . . ."

"Who?"

"Well, uh, at least I think it was a guy. I suppose it could have been a woman, but . . ."

"What kind of car?"

"Medium. Dark, and . . ."

"How much have you had to drink, buddy?"

"Uh, nothing, honest . . ."

"It's probably kind of dumb to ask if you got the license number, but just in case . . ."

"Uh, well, no, I didn't."

"Do you have a history of mental illness?"

"Uh . . ."

"Drugs?"

"Listen, now. I work for the *Chronicle*. There's somebody trying to kill me, really."

"Press card?"

"Uh, well. I haven't been working there much lately and . . ."

"Uh-huh."

"Look, my name's Paul McDonald and . . ."

"Yeah, yeah, we got your driver's license. Move along now."

I moved along into the elevator that comes down to the underground garage to take prisoners to jail. Bet you didn't know about that, did you? That's why you never see anyone in handcuffs walking up the steps and standing around waiting for the lobby elevator. This way it's ever so much more discreet. And a good thing, too, because I was currently in handcuffs.

"Like I was saying, my name's Paul McDonald, and if you'd just mention it to . . ."

"Yeah, the mayor. Maybe the D.A. Now that we know it wouldn't be name-dropping, we'll say hello to all your friends in high places."

". . . to Inspector Howard Blick."

Silence.

"Homicide Inspector Howard Blick."

"You one of Blick's guys?"

"Something like that."

It seems they thought I was a murderer. Great little attention-getter.

They threw me in a cell for a while, and then they came

and got me and let me out with a couple of moving violations, which I suppose I deserved.

"You talked to Blick?" I said.

"Yeah." The old cop letting me out was in a lousy mood.

"And he sent his love?"

"He said it was gonna be his misfortune to deal with you later, but if we didn't get you off these premises before he had to come in again, he was gonna personally bomb the building, just because he was sure you were in it."

"He's like a father to me."

Clang went the jail door behind me. It was a sweet sound.

CHAPTER 20

Sardis was sweet, too. It was nearly ten o'clock by the time I got home, and I hadn't had a chance to call her, but she didn't seem at all upset. She was curled up on her brown velvet sofa, Spot on her chest and a book in her hand, the very picture of serenity. Her rose caftan had crept up, revealing a pair of the prettiest calves in San Francisco. Every time I saw these legs I had trouble breathing right.

She got up and kissed me lazily and didn't ask why I was so late, but of course I could hardly wait to tell her. I did it while we put together a late supper of leftovers from Sardis' opus of the night before.

In fact, I caught her up on everything, including the burglary and my date with Marilyn. We chewed it all over, but didn't come up with much. At that point there was only one thing to come up with, really—the whereabouts of Lindsay Hearne.

"You know her," I said. "Think. Where would she go? What would be in character?"

"It's not in character for her to commit kidnap in the first place. Or for that matter to want to be with Terry, particularly."

"Terry's dying."

"Okay, that means she feels guilty and maybe maternal. The Lindsay I know is nothing like that."

"Dammit! Okay. Suppose it were you. What would you do?"

"I don't know. I guess I'd be thinking about trying to get Terry well. I'd probably try a cancer quack."

"But she didn't. So assume she doesn't believe Terry can get better. She's actually accepted the fact that she's dying."

Sardis shrugged. "I don't know. I guess I'd want her to have a good time the last few months of her life. I'd try to give her everything she wasn't going to get later. Just a real good time, that's all. Like that TV show—*Run for Your Life*."

I stared at her. In awe. "Disneyland," I said.

"Sure, why not?"

"It was there all the time. So obvious."

"What?"

"Lindsay even said it to Marilyn—she said she wanted to spend some tme with her, to take her to Disneyland, things like that. That's probably *exactly* what she wanted."

"Wait a minute. I thought she wanted to get Terry away from Jacob, who was endangering her health."

"I think she did. I think that's why she snatched her. But suppose she hadn't had to snatch her. Suppose Jacob had just said, 'Okay, Lindsay, take her for a while. Have a good time.' Then she would have taken her traveling, right? So just because she snatched her is no reason not to do what she would have done anyway."

"It would be safer, even," said Sardis, getting into the spirit. "Because she'd be constantly moving. No one would know where to look because by the time they looked there, she'd be gone."

"Sure. Disneyland, first stop, maybe. Or maybe somewhere else first, since she mentioned Disneyland to Marilyn. Where else would you go?"

"The Grand Canyon."

"Absolutely. Glacier National Park. Yellowstone."

"A mule ride on Molokai."

"A dude ranch."

"Skating at Rockefeller Center."

"Lots of things in New York—the Empire State Building, Radio City Music Hall."

"Europe, do you think? India? The Taj Mahal?"

I thought about it. "No. I doubt Terry has a passport, for one thing, and if they applied for one, they might get nabbed. For another thing, I don't think Lindsay would want to go too far from UC Medical Center and Dr. Rumler. Terry's not going to stay in remission forever, and I suppose she could become very ill very suddenly. Lindsay wouldn't want to risk being in a strange place."

"So all we have to do is comb this country."

"Oh, God!" I said despairingly. "They could be traveling under new names; they could have changed their appearance—God knows what they might have done."

"So where do we start?"

I thought about it. "I'm damned if I know. We could ask park rangers if they've seen them, I guess."

"Oh, come on."

"Well, I know there's a better way. I just haven't thought of it yet."

"Why don't we sleep on it?"

"Sleep on it?" Sardis had just thrown another puzzling element into the bubbling brew I already had in my head.

193

"Yeah. Sleep on it. You know." She made a pillow out of her hands and put her head on it.

"I don't think so. I'm not tired."

Only exhausted. For some reason I just didn't want to get in bed with Sardis right then.

"Okay," she said. "You mull it, Marlowe. Good night."

I mulled it for a while, but I couldn't get anywhere. I followed her to bed and she rolled into my arms: "Want me to rub your back?"

"Sure."

She was good at it. Not only that, she obviously enjoyed it. I could tell she was getting aroused; I wasn't, but I wanted to be. Making love, I thought, would make us both forget this whole mess for a while. All I needed was a little encouragement. I rolled over on my back to give her the idea, and she was quite a quick study. She got the idea and she encouraged. But nothing happened. Meaning, to put it bluntly, I couldn't get it up. A most embarrassing situation.

"Uh, gee," I said, or something along those lines. "I guess I'm kind of under pressure. I mean, this has never happened before."

Only with Maureen, anyway.

"It's nothing," she said. "Don't you ever have writer's block?"

"What does that have to do with it?"

"Well, it's the same thing. You've got lover's block."

"Oh." Oddly, I was relieved. "Does it ever go away?"

"Sometimes." She put her head on my chest and closed her eyes.

I couldn't go to sleep, so I thought about the case. It was a way to keep from thinking about what had just happened. I thought the whole thing through, going over each separate incident, right from the moment Jack told me about it.

My mind kept going back to something that had happened the day before. It was something to do with the case, but it was an incident so trivial I couldn't believe it meant anything. It had to, though—otherwise, why would it keep coming back?

I fell asleep.

CHAPTER 21

I think I slept about three minutes. I woke up because Sardis was beating on my chest and saying my name. I knew, of course, what had happened. The murderer had somehow got into the apartment. This was making Sardis nervous, which was why she was waking me up, but I knew, naturally, that there was nothing to fear, as he was making love with Maureen. I tried to tell this to Sardis, but she kept saying, "Wake up."

So I woke up even more and she said, "I know where she is."

"Lindsay?"

"Who'd you think?"

I couldn't say "Maureen," so I kept quiet.

"We have an old friend from college who owns a dude ranch."

"A dude ranch?"

197

"Wouldn't that be a natural place to take a kid? You said so yourself."

"Did I?" I come awake fairly slowly.

"Yes, when we were thinking of places they might have gone. You said it and I forgot about it and then something kept bothering me. I couldn't get to sleep."

"I can understand that."

"Well, it was what you said. About a dude ranch."

"Oh."

"Our friend Rachel Carroll, from Newcombe, lives on one. And she has a kid about Terry's age. And here's the best part—the place is practically inaccessible."

"Oh again."

"I was thinking that even if she's traveling around to every amusement park in the country, she has to have a sort of home base. Rachel's the person she'd go to. I'm sure of it."

"Was she close to Rachel in college?"

"Like that." Sardis crossed her fingers. That night she was big on hand signals.

"Where is this place, anyway?"

"Lassen County."

"Why don't we call her?"

"Now?" Sardis looked at her bedside digital clock. "It's one-fifteen."

"Okay, let's wait till morning. Three people have been killed, but probably no one else'll buy the farm for the next few hours."

She was already dialing. I listened.

"Rachel? Darling, it's Sardis. No, nothing's wrong. I mean, a lot of things are wrong, but I'm not sick or anything. Listen, I have a very important question to ask you. It really is a matter of life and death, okay? Rachel, is Lindsay there? . . . She's not." There was a pause. "I need to know because things are very fucked up here. I've really got to talk to her. . . . Okay, dear, I know you'd help if you could."

Sardis hung up. "She's there."

"I thought she wasn't."

"Rachel didn't sound like herself at all. Lindsay must have told her under no circumstances to tell anybody where she is. All Rachel asked was why I needed to know, not why I thought she'd be there or what was going on or anything. I think she thought Jacob was holding me hostage or something."

"You should have told her about Brissette and Tillman."

She pondered. "Maybe. But look, in the morning Rachel will tell Lindsay I called and she'll probably call me."

"We can't take the chance. How long does it take to get there?"

"About six or eight hours. The roads are unbelievable."

"Let's fly."

"Are you nuts? There's no way to . . ."

She stopped, because this time I was already dialing, calling my friend Crusher Wilcox, amateur pilot and small plane owner.

"Crusher? . . . No, nothing's wrong. I just need your help, that's all. I have to get to Lassen County tonight."

"You want to borrow my car?"

"No. I want you to fly me there. A friend and me. I'll buy the gas."

He brightened. "Oh, *fly*. Let me see—the forecast says, umhmm. The hmm, something or other."

He didn't really say that. It's just that when Crusher starts talking about flying, it all sounds like that to me. I think he was figuring out if the weather was going to be good enough to do it.

"Looks good," he said finally. "Where, exactly, do you want to go?"

"Just a second." I asked Sardis.

"Little Valley," she said. "Near there, anyway."

"What else is it near?"

"Nothing, really. Little Valley's on the edge of Lassen National Forest. Susanville's not *too* far."

I spoke to Crusher. "Near Lassen National Forest. It doesn't bode too well for an airport."

"This could be interesting," he said. "Very interesting indeed. Meet me at the airport in forty-five minutes."

He meant the Oakland Airport, where he kept his Cessna 182, and we were there with five minutes to spare, even though we'd taken time to throw a few clothes in a bag.

One thing I'll say about Crusher—he's always ready to fly. Any time of the night or day, all you have to do is say the word and he's Mr. Enthusiasm. He'd already gassed up and figured out a flight plan.

You can't talk in a small plane until you're five miles away from the airport, because this might distract the pilot from hearing the tower. So we were pretty well on our way by the time Crusher noted cheerily that weather conditions weren't exactly ideal, but he was sure we'd be all right. Quite a challenge, he seemed to think.

I asked him where we were going to land, figuring he'd looked up the nearest tiny airport in some pilot's manual or other. Good old Crusher. He'd probably have it all figured out.

"Let's see." He glanced at his watch. "It's nearly three now. I think it'll be okay. Yep. Should be okay. It'll probably take us a couple of hours to get there."

"What does the time have to do with it?"

"Can't land until dawn."

"How come? If you can take off at three A.M., why can't you land when you want to?"

"No lights. Or anyway, maybe no lights. Fall River Mills is the closest airport to Little Valley and who knows what they've got there? See, a lot of little airports don't

200

have anybody there at night, so they turn the lights off. On the other hand, some of them have a great thing—you can turn on the runway lights by punching your microphone button five times. Very ingenious system. Not sure about Fall River Mills."

"So what are we going to do?"

"Well, let's see, how close are you going to Little Valley?"

"About three or four miles," said Sardis. "Southwest."

"No good for Fall River Mills. It's a good fifteen miles away. I can set you down within a mile or two. I mean, who's going to be driving in a national forest at dawn?"

"What difference does that make?"

"That and the light are the two crucial factors. If it's dark, we can't see to land; and if there's cars on the road, we can't land on top of them."

"You mean we're gonna do it in the road?"

"Like I said, it'll be a challenge."

We encountered, as the airlines say, unexpected turbulence—unexpected by Sardis and me, at least. I guess Crusher pretty well figured on it because the four-seater was well-stocked with barf bags.

Sardis only threw up once. I regret to say that my record was somewhat worse. My nerves get a bit frayed when I'm in a plane that feels like it's being hammered apart by Thor and half a dozen of his minions.

But do you think that bothered Crusher? The truth is, I don't know. Either he kept up a line of relaxed patter to keep our spirits up or it didn't faze him.

He told Sardis how he got his nickname (shortened from Bus Crusher after a traffic mishap involving a public conveyance), and in between heaves we told him why we wanted to go to Lassen National Forest in the middle of the night.

He nodded, as if three murders and a missing TV personality came along every day. He's a mucky-muck at a

201

Fortune 500 company, so I guess he sees dirtier stuff all the time. Anyway, he sure took it calmly. He had only one question: "Think Lindsay and the kid'll come back with you?"

"Who knows?"

"Because if they do, I can't give you a ride back. Plane only holds four," he said apologetically. "But if it's just the two of you, or maybe three, I could go to Fall River Mills and wait for you."

"Great. We'll phone you there."

The hammering stopped after an hour or two and we were feeling relatively calm when we began circling the area of the forest where Crusher thought we could land.

It was dawn then, or just beginning to be, and I didn't think I'd ever seen anything so pretty. The first pink streaks, the redwoods, your regulation dawn—but somehow, after that flight, the freshness of it was plain moving. No other word for it.

On the third circle, we found a great little landing strip, or so Crusher seemed to think. It looked to me like a tiny band of asphalt between two rows of giant redwoods. If you've ever flown into the Hong Kong airport, you know the thrill of squeezing between two rows of skyscrapers to land. This was a lot like that, as far as the thrills went, only it was eerily beautiful.

The amazing thing about redwoods is how still they can seem. They don't have leaves that flutter in the wind or branches that stick out at this angle or that. They just stand there, tall and conical and green and primeval. If you've ever been to Wall Street on a weekend, when it's uninhabited, you have an idea how eerie extremely tall things can get. When they are beautiful tall things, you just naturally get an eerily beautiful effect.

Crusher made what I called a perfect landing, and what he called an "A-minus" one. I thanked him, heaped praise all over him, and asked him the troubling question that had nagged at me for the last couple of hours: "What do we do now?"

"Almost forgot. Here's a map for you." And he taxied down the runway, or what passed for it.

It looked to be about a five-mile hike to Little Valley. Sardis said it was another seven miles to the Lazy C Ranch, which is what Ms. Carroll called her establishment. If we wanted to take the ranch by surprise—which we did—we could hardly ask them to send a car. So we started walking, thinking maybe we could reassess things once we got to Little Valley.

We'd gone about a mile and a half, I'd say, when a man in a truck stopped us. He was a ranger, and feeling macho: "What do you folks think you're doing here?"

I did the talking. "Walking to Little Valley. Are we going the right way?"

"How'd y'all get here?"

"Friend dropped us off."

"Friend dropped you off. Do tell."

I didn't really understand why a forest ranger was harassing two harmless citizens on a public road, and I said as much.

"Don't get smart with me, buddy," he said. "Let's see what's in that bag."

"What? Are you crazy?" I didn't get it at all.

But Sardis apparently did. "You think it's dope of some sort, don't you? Here, let me show you."

And she opened it up, something I wouldn't have done in a million years. It was the right thing to do.

"Oh, listen, I apologize. I mean, you see a private plane land on one of these roads this time in the morning, you got to figure something funny's going on. Private planes mean dope, you know what I mean?"

Now that he mentioned it, I did. He kept on talking: "But now that I think of it, they'd be picking something up or taking it away, and they'd have cars and every kind of thing. It'd never just be two people walking along with a suitcase. No way that fits in."

He paused a moment. "It was a wonderful thing to see, that plane. Just went down right between the redwoods and landed. I mean, I didn't see the part when it actually touched down because the trees were in the way, but it's gone now so it didn't crash. You folks didn't happen to see it, did you?"

"Not exactly," said Sardis. "We were in it at the time."

"No shit! That was you folks?"

Of course he'd known all the time that it was. Now that he'd decided we weren't dope distributors, he was curious as hell about who we were and what we were up to. So I didn't see why we shouldn't tell him. Maybe he'd be so grateful he'd be willing to do us a favor in return.

"Sardis," I said, "I think we should tell him about it." I spoke with what I hoped was an air of great solemnity.

Sardis nodded, equally solemn.

"Maybe you could help us," I said to the ranger.

"Why, sure. I'll be glad to." He paused and thought it over. "Uh . . . help you with what?"

"Well, you're probably wondering why we landed a plane in here at dawn—I mean, you probably think it's a little eccentric, right?"

"It don't happen every day, exactly."

I looked at him for a long time, hoping to give the impression I was sizing him up. "Can we trust you?" I said, after one of the longer pauses in recorded history.

"Well . . . sure."

"It's kind of secret."

"Hey, anything I can do, you know? Like I said, you can trust me."

"I'm Paul McDonald," I said, "and this is Sardis Kincannon."

"Bill Carver."

204

"Bill, I work for a private detective. Miss Kincannon's got a friend in trouble."

Sardis looked very sad.

"You see, Bill, the guy I work for—the detective?"

Bill nodded.

"Murdered."

"No!"

"I'm afraid so. And he's not the only one. Three people have died so far. So you see why we're so worried about Miss Kincannon's friend." I paused for dramatic effect. "And her little girl."

"Yeah. I guess I do."

"I mean, you might think the plane was a little melodramatic, but there's just no time to be lost. Because we have to get there first. Do you understand?"

"I think I do. Because if *they* get there first . . ." he drew a finger across his throat.

"That's right."

"The only thing is . . ."

I was ready for him. I interrupted him in mid-sentence. "I know. I know. How do you know we're not *them*? Well, listen, that's easy. You don't think we'd try an operation like this without friends, do you? No. The authorities know what we're doing. We have allies. Have to in this business or you don't survive, know what I mean?" I caught a glimpse of Sardis and saw her mouth twitching. "So look, here's what you do. I'm going to give you a phone number. It's the number of the *Chronicle* in San Francisco—ever read the *Chron?*"

"Never miss it."

"Well, you call this number and you ask for the city editor—guy named Joey Bernstein. He'll back us up. But listen, here's the important thing. If they try to give you to somebody else, some assistant deskman or something, don't talk to him, whatever you do. It's very, very

205

important to keep this quiet, you understand? I mean I can't overstress the importance . . ."

"You can trust me, Paul."

"Good. Because they *will* try to foist you off on somebody else." I looked at my watch. "Joey won't be in for three hours yet. So what you have to do, you have to say it's an emergency and ask them to get Joey at home. He'll take the call if you use my name."

"Gee, I hate to wake him up."

"Hey, Bill, I do too, but this is a matter of life and death, you know? I mean, if anything was ever that, this is. Look, Joey likes to sleep late as much as the next guy, but if he thought he could save a woman's life . . ."

"Paul," said Sardis, "you're forgetting Terry."

". . . the lives of a woman and her child, what choice do you think he'd make? I mean, what kind of a man do you think he is?"

"Well, I think we can have it both ways."

"Beg pardon?"

"Look, I believe you folks. You folks seem like real sincere people to me. What can I do for you?"

"Do you think you could give us a lift to Little Valley? I think we could get a taxi or something there."

"Hah! You kiddin'? This time of the morning? Now, hop in. Where we goin'?"

"Lazy C Ranch."

So that's how we got a ride to Rachel's. Bill made one quick stop at the ranger station and got us to the Lazy C by 6:30.

Rachel's ranch house was Spanish style, badly run-down for a place that took in paying guests, and completely charming, to my mind. Nobody was up but the dog. He went for my left heel.

"Sit, Ishi," said Sardis. "Come. Heel. It's Aunt Sardis, dammit. Down, you sucker. Paul, don't!"

She squealed the last just as I raised the suitcase to bean

him with, and I would have hit him a good one except that Rachel, aroused by the ruckus, appeared and called him off.

She was a handsome woman, dark with green eyes. Sardis had told me she'd been running a ranch alone for the last two years—ever since she caught her husband with one of the wranglers and tossed him out. The Lazy C did have some female wranglers, it seemed, but that wasn't the kind Rachel's husband was fooling around with. According to Sardis, Rachel said if it had been a woman, she would have kept him around without too many hard feelings. But she didn't like having her cowboy illusions shattered.

Anyway, she looked like the kind of woman who could run a dude ranch and raise a kid alone. She had great shoulders.

"Sardis, darlin'!" She came outside in her blue fleece robe and enfolded Sardis. "I'm sorry, honey. Lindsay was *real* firm on the subject of not lettin' anyone know where she was. *Real* firm. You just never know what Jacob might do and I thought maybe . . . I mean, I just didn't know. I'm real sorry, honey."

"Thank God," said Sardis. "She's here, then?"

"Why, no. No, she isn't."

CHAPTER 22 "Shit.

Goddammit. Fuck!" I looked around for Ishi, thinking to kick him to let off steam, and as you know, I'm a sucker for animals.

"Who's your friend?" said Rachel.

Sardis blushed. "He's not *too* bad when you get to know him. I mean, he doesn't spit or fart or anything. Once he even opened a door for me."

I felt like an ass. "Sorry, Rachel. I'm just feeling kind of frustrated. My name's Paul McDonald."

"You're kidding. Paul McDonald, the writer?"

Good lord! A fan. Susanna was the first one I'd ever met and now here was another. It was too good to be real.

And it wasn't. I was busy pinching myself while Rachel had the bad manners to explain: She'd seen my story about Jacob.

I liked her anyhow. She fed Sardis and me a ranch-style breakfast of pancakes and sausage while she told us about

Lindsay. It seems we'd guessed exactly right. Lindsay was using the Lazy C as a home base, but she was traveling around a lot with Terry. Terry seemed quite well and Lindsay wanted her to have a good time while she still could. So they were gone most of the time. So far they'd been to Disneyland and Yellowstone and now they were at the Grand Canyon.

Or more specifically, they were aboard a raft on the Colorado River. They'd left two weeks ago, and there was no way to get in touch with them for another week.

"No way in hell," as Rachel put it.

"You're sure?"

"No question, honey. I know because of Terry. Lindsay was real worried she'd get sick on the river, but she decided to go ahead and take the chance."

"How about helicopters? Maybe we could hire one to lower us down."

"Honey, I don't see how. I mean, if the raft's movin' along with the river, how's it gon' hold still long enough for that?"

There had to be a way. I was trying to think of it while Sardis asked Rachel if she could make a phone call and then went off to do it.

She came back looking all tense, as if a lot depended on something or other. "Rachel. What day did Lindsay and Terry actually get on the raft?"

"About a week ago, I think. They were gonna drive around and do a lot of sightseein' the first week."

"The raft must have left from Lee's Ferry."

"It was Lee's Ferry. I remember specially because Lindsay had to look real hard to find a raftin' company that would take a kid that young. Finally found one there."

Sardis spoke with infinite patience. "Do you remember the day the raft trip started?"

"Well, let's see. They left . . . well, it was about a week and a half ago, actually on a Monday. They had a

210

week before the raft trip. Today's Thursday, so that means . . ."

"Last Monday. Did they leave Monday?"

"I do b'lieve they did." Rachel looked puzzled. "What difference does it make?"

Sardis' tense face relaxed. She went positively radiant with relief. "I think we can catch them."

She was too much, that Sardis.

"I just called the Grand Canyon Visitors' Center. They said we can flag them down when they pass Phantom Ranch."

"No!"

"It takes six days to get there from Lee's Ferry, so that gives us till day after tomorrow."

"That should be plenty of time."

"It's barely enough. It means we have to get there today. Because it takes a whole day to get down to the ranch."

Rachel sighed deeply. "Y'all can't make it."

"Why not?"

"You got to get from here to someplace with an airport—nearest place is probably San Francisco. Then you gotta fly to Flagstaff and then get from there to the place to start hikin' in. And it'll take you all day just to get back to San Francisco."

Sardis smiled. "Uh-uh. I just called Crusher at Fall River Mills. He's gassing up now."

"What about your job?"

"I called in sick."

"Let's get going."

"I've still got another phone call to make." And she went off to call a neighbor to feed Spot for a few days.

Rachel took us to Fall River Mills, said, "Y'all come back," and bumped back down the road in her pickup.

"Sardis, sugar," I said, "why don't y'all talk like that?"

She said, "Never use y'all in the singular."

"Let's go!" Crusher wasn't only gassed up, he was

211

revved up as well. I never saw a man so eager to leave the planet.

He looked at his watch. "Even with a gas stop we'll make it by early afternoon."

"To Flagstaff?"

"Hell, no. Right to the South Rim. That's where you want to go, isn't it?"

"Not if you have to make another unconventional landing."

"You didn't like that landing? Most fun I ever had."

"It was great. I just don't want to get in trouble with the law and end up in some Arizona jail."

"Relax. There's an airstrip."

We may not have relaxed, but at least we didn't throw up anymore. The weather was wonderful—no challenge at all for Crusher—so it was a pretty flight. And if I thought landing at dawn in a redwood forest was impressive, I was a callow pup. Redwood forests are tall and attractive, but so am I. You want to be impressed, go to the Grand Canyon. I was in the front of the plane and Sardis was sitting in the back, but that didn't stop us from holding hands on the way down. We weren't scared; it was just lonesome with that much beauty around.

Crusher seemed kind of depressed there was no place else to fly us to, but then he got the idea he could just take a joyride around the canyon and the state and maybe the whole Southwest, and that cheered him up. He called his office and said he'd be back next week. Then he had a hot dog and a Coke and flew off again, leaving me wishing there was something in life I loved as much as he loved flying. A woman, maybe. Maybe Sardis. But the thing was, I had lover's block.

So it looked like I wasn't going to be soaring off into the wild blue. I was going to have to live with a cat and pound out mysteries that didn't sell and occasionally do a job of work to support both cat and habit.

It was a grim thought, and here I was at the Grand Canyon with a beautiful, wonderful woman. Who in the world wouldn't envy me? So of course cooler heads prevailed and I quit thinking grim thoughts. It was just for a moment, watching Crusher fly off, that I had that funny twinge.

Then I got busy and started having a good time. But first I called Joey Bernstein. As usual, he was thrilled to hear from me:

"McDonald, goddammit, who authorized expenses to Lassen County?"

"Lassen County? I'm not in Lassen County."

"Some forest ranger woke me up at six A.M. to say you were."

Oho. So young Bill Carver wasn't as gullible as he seemed. He'd called Joey when he stopped at the ranger station, which wasn't a bad move at all—if we'd been the mysterious "them," he'd have had us cold.

"McDonald? You there?"

"I was just trying to figure out the best way to break the news. Listen, forget about Lassen County. I don't need expenses for that, okay? I mean, my overtime'll probably cover it. Don't you worry your pretty head."

"Overtime! What the hell are you getting at, McDonald?"

"How do you feel about the Grand Canyon?"

"I'm gonna tell you something, Paul. This better be good. That's all I'm gonna tell you. Now start talking."

I started talking. Joey was a convert by the time I got to the unauthorized highway landing. He was beside himself when I mentioned flagging Lindsay down on her raft. I told him Sardis had come along because no way was Lindsay going to talk to a perfect stranger, but he didn't buy it. He just couldn't understand why anyone in the world wouldn't want to talk to a reporter any time of the day or night. Newspaper folks are funny that way.

Anyway, we haggled for a while and I said if he felt that way about it, I'd have to tackle Lindsay by myself. I think he was ninety percent sure I was bluffing (which I was), but he wanted the story so bad he lost his judgment and agreed to pay expenses for both of us.

Sardis hadn't expected that.

"Well, as long as you came all this way, it's the least we can do," I said. "I mean, I want you to know I really appreciate what you're doing."

"But, Paul—" she looked bewildered. "I'm not doing it for you. I'm doing it for Lindsay."

Of course she was. I'd forgotten that, and that's yet another example of how self-important a reporter on a story gets.

Next we went to work on the Lindsay-catching logistics. Here's how it all shook down: We'd stay that night at the Grand Canyon Auto Cabins, auto or not, and the next day we'd take the mule train to Phantom Ranch.

The Bright Angel Trail is eleven miles and the Kaibab Trail is eight miles, so you *can* hike down—the only problem is that you have to hike up again and who needed that?

The next twenty-four hours were among the finest of my misspent life. I was overwhelmed by the beauty of the place and feeling very close to Sardis.

We wandered around, hand in hand, for a little while, but we'd been up all night the night before, so pretty soon we went back to the Auto Cabins for a nap. We made love before we went to sleep and again when we woke up and yet again when we came back from dinner. There was something very relaxing about being on the rim of the deepest chasm in the world.

As I was drifting off to sleep, I thought happily that this night had certainly been different from the one before. My relationship with Sardis didn't make me feel so pressured here; despite the seriousness of our mission, it felt rather

214

like we were on vacation and I wished it could go on awhile. Recalling the ignominious night before, I remembered that the mind had worked about as well as the body—there had been something, something about the murders that I couldn't get the hang of. I went back over it.

It was something trivial; something someone had said. I could hear the words, but couldn't see that they meant anything. It was like one of those puzzles in which you have to guess what's wrong with this picture. You stare and stare at it and it looks fine. Then, in a split second, the thing that's wrong sticks out like it's three-dimensional, and you can never look at the picture again without seeing it. That's what happened that night at the Auto Cabins. I remembered the incident and it looked fine. Until suddenly I saw what was wrong with it. I went to sleep knowing who the murderer was.

If you haven't ridden a mule to Phantom Ranch, do it. You start off very straight down a long plateau, where the rock is red and gold and very beautiful. Then you enter the eerie inner gorge and the weather changes. It's sunless there, and surprisingly cool, with only a narrow slice of sky. For the first time, you can hear the sound of the river.

Near Phantom Ranch, though, the river is quiet, and the ranch is tucked into a valley full of cottonwoods. I think that ride might be a great opportunity for a spiritual experience if it weren't for the pain. It's pretty hard to leave the physical plane with your ass throbbing.

But a sore bottom is a small price to pay for the pleasure of the trip. It was easy to forget Jack and Brissette and Tillman and all the rest of the whole Koehler mess, and we did. We were happy together.

That day and the next one, when we did nothing but sit on the bank of the river, are a rosy-gold blur to me. We sat there on our damaged fannies and watched raft after raft

215

float by, and there seemed no higher purpose mankind could serve. And then, all of a sudden, Sardis was on her feet and yelling. She was wearing shorts and I was momentarily distracted by the sight of her legs.

Then I saw Lindsay Hearne in a raft coming towards us. I got up and started yelling too. Lindsay looked panicked.

Sardis was hollering something about an emergency, and I chimed in. I felt very sorry for Lindsay. The day she'd left the Lazy C Ranch, Jack Birnbaum was dying in my living room. Even if she were still in the *Chronicle* circulation area the next day, his obit would have meant nothing to her. She had no way to know his death was connected with her or that he was even looking for her. By the time her lover and her former lover died, she would have been too far away for the news to reach her. One death was supposed to be an accident and one a suicide, so they wouldn't have been news outside of San Francisco.

While Brissette and Tillman were dying, she was sightseeing with her daughter, maybe looking at oversized cacti and Indian artifacts, having a few last days of happiness before a terrible sadness would come. And now we were bringing her another sadness. Or perhaps two. If you got news of two deaths at once, was that two sadnesses or just one bad one? I mused on it a bit and forgot to yell "emergency," but the fellow steering the raft was headed toward shore. They were going to stop.

Lindsay was newly tanned and incredibly beautiful, in that way that women are after a week in the sun. But she looked very scared.

She jumped out of the raft and embraced Sardis, holding her tight for a minute or two. Then Terry got out and kissed her auntie as well. She looked fine—like any healthy seven-year-old.

I realized I was relieved. I'd expected her, I guess, to be pinched and scrawny-looking, maybe have some of her hair missing.

"What's wrong?" said Lindsay. "Is it Jacob?"

Sardis shook her head, her eyes filling with tears as she realized what she had to tell Lindsay. "No," she said. "But it's real bad. Can we go somewhere and talk?"

"Sure." Lindsay turned around and spoke briefly with the captain, or whatever they call raft executives. Then she spoke with one of the women on the raft. She told Terry to stay with the woman. "I have an hour," she said to us. "Who's this man?"

Sardis told her and we went to a quiet place on the river to talk. We started with the worst first, telling her that Brissette and Tillman were dead and letting her cry and try to absorb the shock before we went on to anything else.

Then I took over and filled in, telling her about working for Birnbaum and getting the files stolen and surviving attempts on my life and believing Brissette was killed because she called him, and Tillman for some other reason that had to do with the case.

Lindsay's grief was at the point where misery gives way to anger. She turned red and hollered, "Jacob!" very loud, and then she hollered it some more, and I think she would have gone on, except that Sardis touched her face, very gently, with one finger. Whoever said you have to slap a hysterical person should consult Dr. Kincannon.

Anyway, Lindsay cried some more, and then she calmed down and began to tell us her story, beginning, like the good reporter she was, with first things first: "Jacob is criminally insane."

"But is he capable of killing three men?" Sardis spoke gently. She didn't want to believe it, I could tell.

Lindsay's eyes filled again. She spoke with the bitterness of a woman betrayed and disillusioned and a bit at her wit's end about the blows life was dealing her: "You know what he was doing with Terry, don't you? If he could do that, he's capable of anything. I found out from her that it was going on—that he was giving her these phony 'treat-

217

ments,' I mean. And then I noticed how yellow she looked. And I fell apart.

"I knew he was crazy. I guess I'd known it for a long time—probably ever since we were first married. But I couldn't quite admit it to myself. I mean, lots of people are eccentric, aren't they?"

"Especially scientists," I said. "People expect them to be."

"Exactly. So this funny quirk or that little oddity gets overlooked because the rest of us expect him to be different. And then when you get into bigger quirks and oddities, you think nothing of it. You're used to expecting their minds to work differently from everyone else's. You say, 'Oh, that's just Jacob; he's a mad scientist.' Only Jacob really is mad. He married me because I had the right genes.

"He used to say that, as some sort of endearment, and I thought it was cute. I thought it was his little joke. And then it turned out he wanted a perfect child and I still never quite realized he was off his rocker. He started pushing Terry, teaching her math when she was three, and things like that, and I just let him. I thought: The man's a genius; Terry probably is too. I liked having a precocious little daughter. But I guess it was too much for her, because we started having behavior problems with her. And I found I didn't like being a mother and didn't want to be one."

She looked straight at me, not at Sardis. Sardis had long since accepted her for what she was, and now she was looking to see if I would. "It's not that I don't love Terry. I love her more than anything and the thought of losing her—I mean, of her dying—is more terrible than the thought of myself dying. But I had her because Jacob wanted her and I've since accepted the fact that I wasn't meant to be a parent. So I got a divorce and relinquished custody.

"That means I haven't been around Jacob very much anymore, but my guess is, it was her illness that pushed

218

him over the edge. I mean, like they used to say, his mind snapped. Or to be more accurate, he lost his already tenuous grasp on reality. He actually thought he was curing her. Do you understand that? The Nobel-winning scientist believes that he has developed a cure for Leukemia. He thinks the FDA is the only thing keeping him from marketing the thing. But the truth is, there is no thing. At least I don't think so."

"You mean you're not sure?"

"I'm pretty sure. Once, when he was still pretty lucid, he told me how it was going to work. He figured it was going to take another two years to get the bugs out—before they could test it on humans. That was less than a year ago.

"Anyway, when Terry told me about the 'treatments,' I confronted him. He acted as if I were out of my mind to doubt him. You know how arrogant doctors are? I mean, you know how they believe they're God? Well, scientists, especially if they've had the kind of recognition Jacob has, are like doctors multiplied by twenty. So suppose a guy like that crosses just a little bit over the line—the line between reality and fantasy, I mean. Can you imagine trying to tell him what's best for his kid?"

"Gives me goose bumps to think about it."

Lindsay nodded. "A real blood-chiller. But, of course, there was always the chance he really *was* right—wasn't crazy, I mean. That he really had discovered a cure."

"So you took Terry to Dr. Rumler to make sure."

She nodded again. "And then I panicked. I called Mike Brissette to ask him what I'd have to do to regain custody. He said it's practically impossible to prove someone's crazy, and particularly someone who's respected in practically every household in the Bay Area. He was very discouraging. I guess that phone call cost him his life." Her voice was shaky.

"You think Jacob killed him?"

219

"Of course. With all due respect, you simply don't seem to grasp the fact that Jacob believes he has a mission to save the world. You've heard of that kind of maniac before, haven't you?" She looked at me cannily. "You were in Guyana, weren't you, Paul? And you knew Jim Jones before that, when he was in San Francisco. Jacob is that kind of nut. Capable of that degree of evil. Believe me."

I nodded and she went on. Sardis looked shocked.

"Anyway, so I decided to try appealing to Marilyn. She's been good to Terry and she isn't a dumb woman." She shrugged. "But it was hopeless. Jacob behaved as if I were the one who was crazy, but Marilyn actually came out and told me I was."

Sardis spoke, for the first time in a while. "But I don't understand. She's a scientist. If he hasn't got the cure, she must know he hasn't got the cure."

"Well, she didn't exactly say he had. She denied that Jacob was giving Terry any treatments at all."

"You told her about the side effects?"

"Yes, and Dr. Rumler and the whole thing. She flat out denied it."

"I still don't get it. Why would she do that?"

Lindsay shrugged. "She's obsessed with him. It's a very sick relationship, I think. He's the better scientist, so she idolizes him, and he's also the world's handsomest man." She shrugged again. "It's sort of sad, really. He needed someone to take care of him and Terry, so he married Marilyn, who adores him and thinks he can do no wrong. She just refuses to see what's happened to him, that's all. He's her whole world, and if she had to stop believing in him, she couldn't make it. So she doesn't see what's happening around her."

"How about Steve Koehler? Did you go to him?"

"Paul, every penny Steve Koehler has is sunk in Kogene, and Jacob is his only asset. Do you think he wants to hear anything against him? All the time I was Steve's
220

sister-in-law, I believe he spoke fifteen words to me. To my knowledge, he has never kissed or hugged his niece. I have never seen him display any emotion except greed, if that's an emotion. Anyway, it's as close as he gets. I'd say he should be eugenically sterilized, except that I'm quite sure he is incapable of so human a thing as fathering a child."

Sardis sucked in her breath. "What happened to these boys when they were kids?"

Again Lindsay shrugged. "Parents died. Raised by relatives who drank and beat them. Passed on to other relatives, then others. The usual stuff."

Sardis nodded. She was very interested in that kind of thing.

But I wanted more details about the case. "Did you have a date with Peter Tillman the night you were supposed to see Marilyn?"

She nodded.

"But you broke it?"

"Not then. I phoned him to say I was meeting Marilyn and asked if we could make it later than we'd originally planned."

"So you saw him?"

"No. As it turned out, I was too upset."

"Did you tell him about the meeting?"

"How could I help it? I blubbered all over the telephone."

"I don't see why Jacob would have killed him for that. I can't see a motive in it."

"Don't you see? It's the same motive for all of them. They all knew he was crazy—Birnbaum, Mike, Pete. That's why he tried to kill you—because he thought you knew too."

"But, Lindsay," said Sardis. "They didn't really know anything. All they knew was, you thought he was crazy."

"So you're wondering why he didn't kill me if that was the motive. He's capable of it, Sardis."

"But the digitalis," I said. "How would he get it?"

"Easiest thing in the world. Haven't you got an aunt with heart trouble? Even I have. And of course Jacob does too. Old Aunt Hallie, the only person who was ever nice to the Koehler boys when they were growing up. When she got old, they moved her out here and ensconced her at Rossmoor, a few doors down from my aunt Katherine. And believe it or not, they both visit her regularly—even that jerk Steve. She's got digitalis lying around like aspirin."

"Does Marilyn visit her, too?"

"Sure. Why?"

"Because if you really believe Jacob could kill three people because they might or might not have thought he was bonkers, and you believe Marilyn is neurotically obsessed with Jacob and would do anything to protect him, the same motive applies for her, doesn't it?"

Lindsay looked confused. "I don't know. You have to be crazy to kill someone, don't you?"

"I don't know, Lindsay. I honestly have no idea. Listen, I hate to be the one to say this, but I'm sure you've already thought of it . . ."

She interrupted me. "I'm not going back with you. I want Terry to have this raft trip."

"But Lindsay—" Sardis looked as if she'd lost her best friend, and I guess she felt that way.

Lindsay interrupted her. "I don't think there's any danger now to anybody but me, and he can't find me on the river."

"What about Paul?"

Lindsay looked shocked, as if she'd forgotten the attempts on my life. She started to cry again. "I have to think. Jacob is Terry's father. I can't imagine yanking her out of the river and up the canyon and back to San

Francisco, just to try to get her father thrown in jail. I just can't . . ."

"I have an idea," I said. "I brought a tape recorder with me. If you'll tape your story, we'll go quietly."

"But, Paul—" Sardis obviously couldn't believe what I was saying, but I knew something she didn't know. I shushed her.

Lindsay looked as if she'd gotten a reprieve from the green room. The truth was, I'd come around to her point of view—she'd be safe on the river, and she might not be if she came back with us. Sardis and I could handle it alone.

CHAPTER 23

"There's something you two should know," I said, and told them about my revelation at the Auto Cabins. With three brains working on it, we put together a much more complete theory than I'd been able to generate alone.

Then we worked out a plan, one that I wasn't crazy about, but they convinced me it was the only way. Lindsay made the tape I'd asked for, and after that, she made a second tape. Then, having heard news of the deaths of two men she was close to and having plotted to trap their killer, all in the space of an hour, she joined her dying daughter and floated off down the Colorado River. She was one brave lady.

Seeing her was inspiring in its way, but it broke the mood of our idyl. We couldn't get out of the canyon till the mule train left the next day, and I was restless. Sardis was too, I guess, but I was too restless to notice.

The part about the plan that I didn't like was that it used

Sardis as bait. I'd agreed to do it on the condition that we first try out our theory on the cops. This galled me because it meant dealing with Blick, but I was worried enough to give it a try.

I called him when we got back: "Howard, this is Paul McDonald."

"Eat shit and die, turkey."

To my everlasting credit I didn't hang up. To this day, when I think about it, my right hand automatically snakes around and pats my lats. "Howard, I've got some very import—"

Click. So much for the boys in blue. I called Susanna Flores.

Then Sardis made a call. I listened to Lindsay's second tape as she played it for the person on the other end of the line:

"Hello, Jacob, this is Lindsay. I believe you killed Jack Birnbaum, Mike Brissette, and Peter Tillman and that this tape could help convict you. I have given Sardis Kincannon another copy in a sealed envelope to be opened in the event that either she or I should die. By the time you get this, the other copy will be in a safe-deposit box."

The tape stopped there. Sardis spoke into the phone: "There's more. Lindsay said it was an insurance policy to keep us safe. I wasn't supposed to listen to it, but I got curious. I don't really think Lindsay's in danger from Jacob, so I don't think she needs an insurance policy, you know? And I thought you might be able to use the tapes. I'm not greedy. I was thinking something in the neighborhood of ten thousand dollars. You could get that much by tonight, easy."

There was a pause.

"Well, five thousand will do for now, then. After all, there are two tapes. One of them will be on sale at midnight at Pandorf Associates. You know the ferry?"

She hung up and grinned at me. "It's set."

We had asked for ten thousand on the theory that it sounded like a reasonable amount for an amateur blackmailer and that at least half of it ought to be readily available on a day's notice. Our nerves weren't good for more than a day.

At ten o'clock we met Susanna Flores at the ferry. She had a cameraman with her, one named Freddie and equipped with a Minicam. I did a stand-up for him. "This is Paul McDonald," I said. "I called Police Inspector Howard Blick today to give him information I thought would be helpful in a homicide investigation. He called me 'turkey' and hung up. I have a tape recording of that telephone call. The police have no part in the 'sting' recorded on this videotape. Susanna Flores of Channel 5 and I hope that it will be valuable evidence in the arrest and conviction of a killer."

The point of that speech was to authenticate the tape. I didn't know whether the thing would hold up as evidence, but I was going to try my damnedest to get it into court. How I was going to get the cops to look at it was another matter—maybe Susanna would have to air it.

Sardis took us to a little room about midway between bow and stern. It was well-appointed with soft, deep plushy gray sofas. One wall was mirrored. "This," said Sardis, "is where we hold the focus groups."

"How's that?" asked Freddie.

"Market research groups. You put a bunch of people in a room and get them to talk about fast-food joints or something. Then the client—McDonald's, say—can find out whether people like their golden arches, or whatever they want to know. We've got microphones in the ceiling, and of course the mirrors are really one-way windows."

"You mean we can tape from the next room?"

"We often do ourselves. It's a great room for extortion, isn't it? Everything all comfy and private. Perfect little false sense of security." Sardis spoke confidently. I wished I felt as upbeat about this crazy caper as she did.

At midnight Freddie, Susanna, and I were in place in the viewing room. Sardis was sitting alone in the reception room, waiting for a killer who was a few minutes late.

At 12:10 the doorbell rang. We heard Sardis answer it and talk to someone. Then we heard their footsteps, and then they entered the room where Pandorf held the focus groups. It was spooky, being able to see them like that— hard to believe they couldn't see back. Sardis' companion looked around the room, appraising it. It seemed to me that our eyes locked for a moment. But that was impossible—I had to tell myself that to keep still.

"No one's on the boat," said Sardis. "But every now and then someone comes down for some reason. No one'll bother us here."

Steve Koehler nodded. "It's a nice room."

"Make yourself at home." Sardis sat down and pointed to a loaded tape recorder on a low table. "There's the tape."

Steve sat down across from her.

Sardis spoke again: "Did you bring the money?"

"Yes." Steve took out an envelope and let Sardis look in it.

She nodded and turned on the tape, the first one Lindsay had made, in which she described Terry's illness, Jacob's phony treatments, the emergency visit to Dr. Rumler, the call to Brissette, the visit with Marilyn, and the talk with Tillman. When it was over, Sardis turned off the machine.

"Lindsay honestly believes Jacob killed those three men," she said. "Only she doesn't want anything to happen to him—at least not right now—because it would be a shock to Terry. On the other hand, she doesn't want to be his next victim. That's why she made the tape."

"If my brother is a killer, perhaps he should be locked up."

"Oh, but he isn't." As she spoke, Sardis took the tape out of the recorder. She kept holding it, hands in lap. "I've
228

thought about it quite a lot and I see how it's possible to come to that conclusion. Because he *is* mad."

"Oh?"

"Of course. How do you explain nearly killing his own daughter?"

"Look, Miss Kincannon, he was doing what he thought best. People don't like to face the truth in situations like that. Everybody's a little bit that way."

"Mr. Koehler, when a Nobel Prize-winning scientist doesn't know what's real and what's not real, he's flipped out."

"Nonsense. There's nothing—"

"Gone bananas, Mr. Koehler. Not playing with a full deck. Besides, a few other things have happened. A man in a stocking mask accosted me and demanded to know where Lindsay was. Susanna Flores got a threatening phone call. Jacob was the assailant and the caller."

She said it confidently, as if she knew it were true.

Actually, it was just part of our theory, but it made sense: Not one but two people wanted to find Lindsay— Steve and Jacob. Steve might be a murderer, but nutty, desperate stuff like that wasn't his style.

"How do you know?" asked Koehler.

"I'm not going to tell you yet. Instead, I'm going to go on with the line of reasoning I followed. I just asked myself a question, that's all—if Jacob wanted to find Lindsay so badly, why would he kill the man he'd hired to find her?"

"You tell me, Miss Kincannon."

"Well, he might if Birnbaum were blackmailing him. Birnbaum tried to blackmail me into giving him information. If he did that routinely, with everyone he investigated, pretty soon he might come upon a piece of information about his client that was worth a lot more than he was getting paid. So maybe he'd blackmail his own client."

229

"That's pretty farfetched."

"Not at all, Mr. Koehler. Only Birnbaum didn't do that. Crazy people don't know they're crazy. What would be the point of trying to blackmail Jacob on that account?"

Koehler shrugged.

"Because that's what he found out about Jacob. Just like Lindsay's tape says. She called Brissette to find out if she could get custody of Terry on grounds that Jacob's marbles were missing. Brissette told Birnbaum about that. He was a coke freak and a politician and therefore vulnerable to blackmail. So Birnbaum didn't have any trouble getting it out of him. Birnbaum didn't even realize how valuable the information was. He didn't know what I know, what the person developing Kogene's new corporate identity would have to know—that your company's going public in a couple of months."

"And you have only one asset, don't you?" Sardis made it a taunt. "Without Jacob Koehler, there really is no Kogene."

"Nonsense. Marilyn's almost as fine a scientist as Jacob is. And we have others—"

Sardis shook her head. "I mean from the point of view of investors. And at this point, your investors are brokers, aren't they? Your investment banker is probably even now putting together a syndicate to offer your stock. The whole deal will fall through if they lose confidence in the company."

"Any company with a good product is going to do well."

"But you don't have one, do you? If word gets out Jacob is bonkers—like in a custody case that gets lots of media play—it's good-bye public stock offering and good-bye Kogene and good-bye every cent Steve Koehler ever made or stands to make."

Koehler's filbert eyes were starting to narrow and make him look mean.

"Birnbaum figured out all that and tried to blackmail you, didn't he? Not Jacob. You. So you just lifted some digitalis from your Aunt Hallie and killed him."

"How do you know about Aunt Hallie?" He sounded panicked.

"Lindsay told me. Birnbaum, incidentally, made kind of a strong case. He had Brissette's story and also Tillman's story to back him up. Tillman had talked with Lindsay the night before she disappeared. All three of them knew Jacob was off his nut, but there was no reason for either Brissette or Tillman to make it public. Probably you would only have had to kill Birnbaum if he hadn't had the reports ghostwritten. When that came out in the paper, you realized Paul McDonald would be able to connect Birnbaum's murder with the job Jacob hired Birnbaum to do. The people whose names Jacob had given Birnbaum would be questioned. So that meant Brissette and Tillman had to be killed. I understand there've been attempts on McDonald's life as well."

Koehler's eyes got even smaller. "Are you working with McDonald?"

Sardis laughed, a horrid mean, contemptuous laugh. I had no idea she was such a good actress. "I don't split with anybody," she said. "After all, I'm not asking for much money, really."

"I don't get this. I thought you were Lindsay's friend."

"Oh, I am. You won't kill her. As long as she thinks Jacob is the murderer, she'll keep quiet about it, for Terry's sake."

"How about after Terry dies?"

"With any luck, she won't until after your public stock offering. By then you'll be long gone."

Koehler looked at her quizzically.

"That's your plan, isn't it? You can't stick around here now. Not with this many murders behind you. Especially considering Kogene's going to fall apart without Jacob—I

231

mean without Jacob's genius. Maybe Marilyn will develop a leukemia cure and maybe she won't. It's too late to wait around and see and you know it. What you're running, Mr. Koehler, is a ghost company. You're hoping nobody catches on to that until you can make away with a few million dollars from the sale of your stock. Which you can't do until you sell it. So all you have to do is keep Lindsay and me quiet until you do."

He sighed and handed Sardis the envelope. "Here's the five grand."

"Thank you." She handed over the tape.

"When can I get the other tape?"

"As soon as you get ninety-five thousand dollars together."

He grabbed her arm. "You bitch." I felt sweat pop out on my forehead. "You said ten thousand for both tapes."

"Let go of me." He did, and she reached for something under the gray sofa she was sitting on. She held the object up so he could see it, then took a step away from him. "The other ninety grand is for this." The object was a tape recorder. She took a tape out of it. "I just made a new one."

Koehler sprang at her, but Sardis was expecting that. She dropped the tape down her blouse and sidestepped away from him. She got into a martial arts pose about as convincing as the one I'd struck in the med center library.

"You're going to have to kill me for it, Mr. Koehler."

"With pleasure, Miss Kincannon," he said, and went for her again. But she wasn't fast enough this time. Her arm went up and his went down under it. He had her by the neck.

If it made me sweaty to see him grab her arm, I could have drowned watching this. I had little prickles all over me and my throat was completely closed—I swear to God, I couldn't breathe at all. I was afraid she was going to die and I was going to have to watch, not knowing what to do. My mind was paralyzed.

Though I have no recollection of it, I suppose it unfroze at some point during the next split second. Because all of a sudden I was in the room with Sardis and Koehler, broken glass flying all around. I landed on one of the sofas and used that as a springboard to Koehler's back. I grabbed his arms with my arms and pried. Sardis squealed.

"Let go, you son of a bitch. Let go!" That was my voice, I think.

He let go and bent over. I somersaulted over him, hitting my head on the side of one of the sofas. That felt like somebody had shoved a conduit through my brain, but I had to get up. If I didn't, Koehler might kill Sardis. If anything happened to Sardis, the world would resemble the Mojave Desert. I couldn't let that happen. The future was up to me.

Those things came to me more as feelings than thoughts, and they came right out of left field. I had no more idea they were somewhere inside me than I'd known I was going to be coming through a window thirty seconds earlier. But there they were, so I got up. Freddie was on his way through the window, the same one I'd crashed through. Sardis was flopping, hard, onto one of the plushy sofas, and Koehler was withdrawing his arm. His hand had a tape in it.

Koehler took off down the corridor, making for the way out. I caught him in the reception room, bringing him down with one of my leftover high school tackles. We rolled over and over, from one end of the small room to the other, neither able to get the advantage.

I had him by the jaw, trying to push it back and snap his neck, and he had me by the jaw-holding hand. I heard a commotion and then someone—Freddie, I realized later— started grabbing at Koehler. Koehler kicked and Freddie went down, knocking over the wood stove.

It separated from its chimney, pouring smoke into the room. The door fell open and burning wood flew out. The drapes caught fire.

Koehler was on his feet before I was, battling Susanna and Sardis, who by now had made it to the reception room. They flailed at him, but he got past and started up the stately wooden stairway to the second deck. The fire roared up past him. We ran back down the corridor, toward the back stairs. Or Sardis did, and I followed. Susanna and Freddie followed me.

The sensible thing to do at that moment would have been simply to go out the front door, leaving Koehler aboard the burning ferry. But I wasn't going anywhere without Sardis. I didn't know what Susanna and Freddie were thinking of, though later it came clear—Freddie had left his Minicam in the focus group room and they weren't going anywhere without it. I found out later they picked it up, then tried to get out the front door like grown-ups, but by that time the fire was blocking the exit. So they ended up tearing up the back stairs somewhat behind Sardis and me.

The air on the second level was already gray with smoke and rapidly turning black. Up there, there was also one sensible course—go out on deck and yell for help. But Sardis, in some primitive frenzy, tore down the corridor, apparently bent on killing Koehler with her bare hands. My plan was to catch her, subdue her, and drag her to safety, by the hair, if necessary.

I was gaining on her, only inches away, when she bumped smack into Koehler, who was running right toward us. The impact spun her toward me and I hit the side of the corridor. She fell back against me, and Koehler, once recovered from the blow, tried to run past us. Sardis stuck out her foot and tripped him. Then she hit the deck, arms flying, boxing his ears, his shoulders, straddling him, pounding him with her tiny fists. Then she started to cough.

I pulled her off him, and once again he started running toward the back exit. The smoke was awful and I was pretty sure we were going to a watery grave if we stayed there much longer, but it turned out there was no choice.

Just as Koehler got a good start, and we had a certain momentum behind him, he hit something and reeled back toward Sardis, who reeled back toward me. All three of us went down. There was an awful crash up ahead as Freddie, the thing he'd hit, reeled back toward Susanna and they both went down.

The smoke was pretty black now, and besides that, it was so irritating you couldn't really keep your eyes open. So I guess Koehler and Freddie didn't see each other when they scrambled up. I could see them only as silhouettes. The silhouettes bumped heads with a nasty whack. Freddie reeled again. Really reeled—went around almost a full turn—and landed in Susanna's arms. She hit the side of the corridor and swayed for a minute. Then her knees buckled and she started sinking, Freddie weighing her down. Koehler zipped past them.

Freddie was coughing and so was Sardis, and so was I by that time. But Susanna wasn't, and that worried me. I wanted to get her out of that smoke fast.

Neither Sardis nor I could catch her before she hit the ground, Freddie on top of her. They completely blocked the corridor, so we couldn't have chased Koehler even if we'd been free to.

I heard the sound of broken glass—Koehler breaking out a window to get outside—and then there was a big whoosh and the fire roared closer, a thick orange cloud sweeping the corridor. Suddenly it was a furnace in there. And the orange cloud was gaining on us.

Freddie got up and made retching noises while Sardis and I examined Susanna. Sardis slapped gently at her face, but it was no good. She'd passed out.

Sardis took her arms and I took her legs, but we couldn't really pick her up. We were coughing too hard and our eyes were tearing too much and we were weak from not getting enough air to breathe. We had to drag her as best we could, Freddie stumbling along behind us, apparently unable to see anything at all now, because we kept hearing him bounce off one wall and then another.

Bits of ash and embers flew around in the thick air—or atmosphere—it wasn't really air at that point. Sometimes the embers landed on us and burned little holes in our clothes and shoulders or backs or wherever they happened to fall. The flames licked us and now and then our clothes caught fire and had to be swatted.

When we got to the window Koehler had knocked out, Sardis heaved Susanna up. But she got only halfway. She dropped her. That wouldn't have been so bad—Freddie and I could have managed—but Sardis' nerves had hit their outer limit. She screamed once, and then started sobbing, sitting down where she was, apparently forgetting Susanna. The flames caught her hair. I had to drop Susanna and beat them out, with Sardis' arms and hands grabbing at mine, trying to flail them away. I should have remembered Sardis' trick for calming hysterics, the way she'd touched Lindsay's face. But I didn't till Freddie leaned over and hit her.

I whirled around. "You son of a bitch."

I went for him, but he caught my wrist. "Easy, man. You get her and I'll get Susanna."

I saw the wisdom of it and reached for her. Suddenly she snapped out of it, or recovered consciousness after being hit, or something. She put her arms around my neck and let me help her stand up. With her face close to my ear like that, she said something into it. "I love you, Paul," she said, coughing out the syllables.

I guess she said it because she thought we were going to die. I thought we might, too, and at that moment I loved her more than I've ever loved anyone or anything.

CHAPTER 24

With Sardis compos mentis again, the three of us lifted Susanna through the window and onto the deck. And then my knees buckled and all of a sudden I was lying down, trying to take in all the air the cool gray city of love had to offer. Freddie and Sardis seemed to be doing the same, and Susanna suddenly made a huge gulping sound. She rolled over on her side and threw up. She made more gulping sounds and pretty soon all four of us were more or less all right, except maybe a little weak.

Freddie apologized to Sardis for hitting her and she said it hadn't really hurt at all and thanked him for it, and about then we remembered we were aboard a burning boat with a murderer. I thought I heard sirens in the distance, but I wasn't sure.

The fire was still crackling and smoke was boiling out of the broken window, but it seemed oddly safe on the open deck after what we'd just been through. Koehler had to be somewhere out there, but it was shadowy and we couldn't see him. We joined hands and ran, single file, to the bow, to see if we could climb down somehow. I got there first and looked over the rail. I could see someone, I thought, in the shadows on the pier. The others joined me.

Marilyn Markham stepped out of the darkness and raised her right arm. "Freeze or I'll blow her head off," she said. She was holding a pistol, pointing it at Sardis. In retrospect, I'm not sure we were in handgun range, but the effect was very impressive at the time. We froze.

In fact, we stayed frozen for a few seconds, just staring at her. Then I heard a noise like *unnnh* right beside me. I jerked my head around and stared into a pair of terrified brown eyes. Sardis'. Koehler was holding her from behind, a knife at her throat. Not a switchblade or a Bowie knife or a machete. A crummy Swiss army knife. But at the risk of repeating myself, the effect was impressive.

Koehler backed Sardis out of range so that none of us could try any funny stuff. He spoke to Freddie: "Dump the camera in the water."

Marilyn trained her gun on Freddie. "No."

Freddie looked from one to the other, like someone watching a tennis match. The sirens I thought I heard were loud and clear all of a sudden.

I heard something else. A thud, like something hitting the deck behind me. It was Sardis. Koehler had pushed her, and now he was running toward the stern. It turned out I was chasing him. I'm not sure how it happened, really, but I was, without any message getting from brain to legs, much the same way I'd jumped through the window and, come to think of it, probably the way Sardis had chased him earlier. My feet were pounding after his. That was all I knew about it.

I was gaining on him, nearly had him, I'm pretty sure, when all of a sudden he went over the rail. All of a sudden I did too. Monkey see, monkey do.

If you've never jumped into 45-degree water from the second-story deck of a large ferry boat in the middle of the night, you've got no right to use the word *shock* ever again. I mean, even if your great-aunt Louise makes out with a Brahma bull or you accidentally stick your tongue in an electric socket. Because that word is mine now.

Pain? All up and down the spine and in the brain and capillaries and hair and fingernails.

Cold? Don't ask.

And fear? As many gallons of it as gallons of water in the Pacific, and each of the latter out to get me.

I registered those things on the downward plunge. When I surfaced, all three of them were centered in my chest. I couldn't breathe. Didn't even know where my nose was. Just knew there was nothing in my lungs like there ought to be. I tried to say Sardis' name, but that was no good because I didn't know where my mouth was. I tried to tread water, but it was the same old story. My arms and legs may have been there, but you couldn't prove it by me.

It must have been another case of body operating without brain, because somehow I stayed afloat and got some air in the old thorax. You'll forgive me if I'm hazy on the details. I was a little on the numb side.

Hearing returned first. I heard sirens and crackling and a lot of yelling and screaming. After a while I got so I could separate the voices doing the screaming. Some were men's voices, hollering things like "ladder" and "hose." One was Freddie's, yelling something about a net. One was a woman's voice—Susanna's, I guess—shouting at Freddie to forget the film and get the fuck down the ladder. One was Sardis', wailing my name. And one was quite near me in the water. It was Koehler's, yelling for help.

"I'm coming," I yelled back. "I'm here."

"He's there," shouted Sardis. "He's there."

"Where?" yelled a male voice.

"I'm here," I yelled, swimming now. Some of the numbness went. Stabbing chest pains took its place.

"Help!" yelled Koehler.

And then he was quiet.

I saw him go down. He was only about ten feet away.

I swam to where I thought he was, but I miscalculated—he wasn't there. I kept swimming around in circles, right around there. Then one of my legs kicked something, just glanced off. My chest hurt like a son of a bitch.

But there was nothing to do but dive, so I did, and came up with Koehler. I got him in some sort of amateur carry and found I could hardly swim with a hundred-eighty pound weight.

"Now what?" I said.

Apparently, I yelled that, too, because someone shined a light on me, a fireman. "Hold tight," he said. "We'll throw you a line."

I faced facts. It wasn't a matter of "hardly"—I couldn't swim at all. I treaded water.

That didn't work out too well, either.

The pain in my chest was killing me, and I was starting to feel faint. I wondered if I should let go of Koehler. My grip started to relax.

But then the fireman did throw me a line, and I grabbed it. I tightened my grip on Koehler.

If I could just get the bastard back on dry land, he was going to fry for three murders. It might be my last revenge, but by God, I was going to have it. That son of a bitch was going to fry. Like bacon. Like burgers. Like liver and onions. He was going to curl up at the corners and sizzle in the pan. I was going to serve him rare, with mustard maybe. Or béarnaise sauce.

I held onto him like death to a dead man, thinking how delicious he was going to be. But I was confused and I knew it. *He* wasn't going to be delicious. *It* was. Revenge. My last revenge.

It ought to be sweet, though. Maybe I'd bake him in a pie.

That wasn't right, either. In California, you didn't fry, you didn't even bake . . . what was it you did? I blacked out.

"Paul, what is it?" Sardis was frantic. "Say it again, Paul. What is it?"

"The green room," I said.

That was it. The gas chamber. I opened my eyes and saw Sardis kneeling beside me. I was lying on the pier. So was Koehler. A resuscitation team was working on him. Suddenly someone hollered again: "He's breathing. It's okay. He's breathing."

Maybe I smiled. At least I tried to. He was going to the green room.

I went to sleep again.

I had a lot of dreams about frolicking animals, some with funny headlights. Someone was singing in my dreams. My mother. The way she used to when I was a kid. It was a song about pretty little horses. "One will be black," she sang, "and one will be white and one will be the color of Paulie's shoe." It was a weird dream for a grown man.

When I woke up, my chest was still killing me. I was in a hospital room. Sardis was there.

"Are you okay?" I said.

She nodded. "Smoke inhalation. Treated and released. The same for Susanna and Freddie. The tape's safe, by the way. Freddie wouldn't go down the ladder until the firemen let him throw the Minicam into a net."

"How about Koehler?"

"He's not going anywhere. He hit the water wrong—broke both his legs. How do *you* feel?"

"I was afraid you'd ask that. I don't think I want to talk about it."

"Oh, don't be a baby."

241

She left and came back with a man in white. "This is Dr. Patella—the resident who took care of you."

Patella grinned. "How you doin', guy?"

"Chest hurts."

"Two broken ribs. No lung puncture. No sweat."

"Yeah?" All of a sudden I felt great. Two broken ribs? Hell, that was nothing. It took a lot to get McDonald down. Raging fires, freezing oceans . . . hell of a lot.

"Yeah. Also, smoke inhalation and exposure. Minor bruises. Nothing much at all. You could walk out of here right now."

"I don't think I want to." I didn't feel that great.

Patella nodded. "Want some Demerol?"

"Don't mind if I do."

He left and a nurse came with a shot. I drifted in and out for the next several hours, mostly sleeping but thinking sometimes, too. That song about the little horses kept running through my head.

Sardis was still there when I came out of it. She said, "Do you feel up to seeing Susanna and Freddie?"

"They're here? Absolutely." I sat up, painfully, while she went to get them. Susanna and Freddie were just the people I wanted to see, along with Sardis. The four of us had things to talk about.

Susanna looked worried, but Freddie seemed on top of the world. "Tape's great," he said. "Couldn't be better. I even got you going through the window. But look here, there's one thing I never understood. How did you know Koehler was the murderer?"

"I could tell by the way he kept trying to kill me."

"Huh?"

"I went to see him at Kogene, saying I was Charlie Haas from the *Wall Street Journal*. When I got home, somebody in a small, light-colored car tried to run me down. It was Koehler."

"You saw him?"

242

I shook my head. "It took me a long time to figure it out. But here's what tipped me—when I went back to Kogene several days later, he didn't say a word about my misrepresenting myself. He just accepted me as Paul McDonald of the *Chronicle*, which means he knew who I was all the time. To take the tour of Kogene, I left my coat in his office. It had all my I.D. in it. I presume he went through it, discovered I was the man in the *Examiner* story—the man he wanted to kill—and set briskly about it."

"I still don't get it."

"My address, you see, wasn't in the *Examiner*. And I'm not listed in the phone book. But it's on my driver's license, which he saw. There's lots of ways to get it and lots of people who could do it, but it comes down to this: If you were president of a multimillion-dollar high-tech company and someone misrepresented himself to get an interview and you found out about it, wouldn't you confront him with it?"

Freddie nodded. "Unless I didn't want him to know I knew."

"Koehler didn't. He slipped when he forgot I was supposed to be Haas, that's all. Anyway, the light car tried to run me down, but a dream I had made me remember something else—a dark car followed me and chased me also."

"So? Does Koehler have two cars?

"I don't know. But I think we've got to check that and a few other things before we turn our case over to Blick." Sardis stopped me. "Too late. Freddie and Susanna just spent several painful hours with him. I have a feeling you and I are next."

"Let's move fast then. It strikes me that several matters are still unexplained. Does everyone agree?"

Everyone did. So I told them my new plan. In minutes they were off, Sardis to Rossmoor, Susanna and Freddie to deal with the Department of Motor Vehicles. I turned over and went back to sleep, thinking I could get to like being an armchair general. The nurse woke me up for another shot of Demerol. That was fine with me.

I was starting to get woozy when Marilyn Markham came in.

"How are you feeling?" She was smiling, looking healthy and pretty in camel slacks and a turtleneck.

"Woozy. I was just thinking about the smart bomb." I was speaking slowly and slurring my words a bit. It was the best I could do.

"You know about that?"

"I've got a primitive idea how it works. What I don't know is why Terry got side effects."

"For the smart bomb to work, the antibody has to be monoclonal, meaning it will bind to only one protein. Ours worked fine on rats and hamsters. But in chimps it binds to three proteins. One of them is the leukemia protein, one is associated with the optic nerve, and one is associated with the liver."

"I don't think I get it."

"We haven't yet done any tests on humans. But it looks as if the drug will cure leukemia, all right. However, it'll make you go blind and destroy your liver as well. Whereas being blind might be preferable to dying of leukemia, the drug will kill you as dead as the cancer will—because you can't live without a liver."

"I thought you told me Jacob wasn't treating Terry. How do you know about the side effects?"

"I lied. I was shocked that you knew. But I didn't know myself until Lindsay told me; I told her she was crazy." She came over and stood by my bed. "Are you sure you're feeling all right? You sound awful."

"Just weak. How close are you to finding the right monoclonal antibody?"

244

"Very close. I'm going to do it." She spoke with an odd, steely determination.

"You know, Marilyn," I said, "I have a feeling Jacob isn't the only mad scientist at Kogene."

She had a hand in her pocket. "What are you talking about?"

"I was kind of wondering what you were doing waving a gun around last night."

"I was doing a little sleuthing of my own. I knew Jacob wasn't the murderer. That meant it had to be Steve. I was tailing him. Isn't that what you call it?"

"You were backing him up."

"What?"

"You knew Jacob was nuts. You couldn't live with him and not know it. That's why you and Steve protected him from the press, why he wasn't even allowed to take phone calls. You had as much stake in the future of Kogene as Steve did. Only all he cared about was the money. You were crazy-determined to finish the project. And I do mean crazy . . ." I closed my eyes a moment to rest. The Demerol was sneaking up on me.

"You were in all the way with Steve," I was barely whispering. "Technically, he killed those guys, sure. But you knew about it and you helped him." That song about the little horses switched on again, somewhere in the back of my brain. "At the last minute you switched horses . . ."

I felt her arm grip mine, and then I felt something like a pinprick. My arm went flying up, instinctively, I guess. The pricking stopped, but Marilyn had a better grip on me now—with both hands. I grappled with her, trying to pull her down so I could bite her or something. I don't know what I was trying to do. I was too woozy. But judging from what happened next, I guess it looked like I was trying to kiss her.

"McDonald, what the hell?" said Howard Blick's voice. And then it said, "Uh, excuse me."

"Help!" I said. "Howard! Help!"

What an unbelievable humiliation. Getting rescued by Howard Blick. It was Sardis' fault too. She was stepping off the elevator on my floor about that time. Thirty seconds sooner and I could have been saved by a lovely maiden instead.

She came in while Blick was still struggling to get cuffs on Marilyn and I was still struggling to stay awake. It took her about two seconds to assess the situation. "Hi, Marilyn," she said. "Aunt Hallie sends her love. She says she hopes you'll come back to see her soon, she enjoyed your last visit so much." She looked at me. "That was a couple of weeks ago, right before Birnbaum died. Neither Jacob nor Steve has been there in six months."

"That clinches it," I said. "Sardis, look on the floor, will you? I think Marilyn dropped a syringe with digitalis in it."

Sardis complied. "It's under the bed."

Blick looked dumber than ever. "What the fuck is this all about?"

"Dr. Markham here helped Steve Koehler kill those folks," I said. "I wouldn't be surprised if she tells you all about it herself."

CHAPTER 25 She did, to avoid being charged with murder one. It went like this: She never was in love with Jacob Koehler at all. Lindsay just thought so because Marilyn's way of controlling his every move was artfully disguised as devoted solicitude. She married him so she could hitch her wagon, if you'll indulge me, to his star. Seems she'd had a little trouble getting her talents recognized, what with being a woman, so she'd decided to turn womanhood to her advantage. Things turned out even better than she'd hoped when Jacob become incompetent, leaving it up to her to develop the smart bomb.

She helped Steve kill the three guys to the extent that she stole the digitalis and lent him her car—a medium-sized dark one. Also, the two of them conspired to protect Jacob. It was she, of course, who talked him out of going public about the kidnapping, but he outfoxed her and did it anyway. She never admitted that she knew—before

Lindsay told her—that Jacob was giving Terry treatments, but I think she did know, at least in some dark corner of her mind.

The night the ferry was gutted, she was a backup, like I guessed, in case something went wrong. She had no idea, of course, that Susanna and Freddie and I would be there, and when she saw us, she momentarily lost her head. That's when she pointed the gun at Sardis. When she took in me and Freddie with his Minicam, she figured out what we'd actually been up to, correctly guessed that the jig was up for Steve, though not necessarily for her, and ordered Freddie not to drop the Minicam. She thought if Koehler tried to implicate her, she could lie her way out of it. But either she hadn't reckoned on Aunt Hallie or she intended to kill her, too.

Who knows? Neither she nor the Koehlers were exactly your average red-blooded Americans. They didn't seem to care how many folks they killed.

As for the rest of us, there's good news and bad news. You can probably predict the bad—Terry died about eight months later. But it was a very peaceful death, at Rachel Carroll's ranch. She just fell asleep one night and didn't wake up.

Jacob's world fell apart when Marilyn and Steve were arrested. He voluntarily checked into a private hospital and Lindsay says he's getting better.

She's back working on Susanna's show and they're both doing great.

Pandorf Associates relocated, but Sardis struck out on her own—she's now a free-lance graphic designer, and she's painting on weekends.

As for me, I wrote a prize-winning series about the foregoing events. Joey Bernstein practically squirmed with delight, but he didn't offer any bonuses for a job well done.

Seeing Sardis nearly get killed that night on the boat had

kind of a sobering effect on me. In a way, I got over my lover's block. That is, I realized I loved her. She still gets on my nerves if she gets too close; let me amend that—if I feel myself getting too close to her. And sometimes she doesn't turn me on. But I should be more precise—I mean, sometimes I don't feel turned on to her.

I used to think if a romance didn't go smoothly, the thing simply wasn't meant to be. But now I think you have to work on these things. So I've taken up meditation. A strange pastime for an ornery guy like me, but I'm certainly no fanatic. If I start feeling too peaceful I call up Blick and trade a few insults.